COURT KEPT

COURT KEPT

COURT HIGH: BOOK 3

EDEN O'NEILL

CHAPTER
ONE

Royal

"Royal, Ramses put in a request... official and everything. He wants to meet with them. He wants to meet with all of us."

My hand punched through wallpaper and thick plaster, the burn immediately shooting through my knuckles and causing about half a dozen Court dudes to look at me.

"What the hell are you fuckers looking at?" I gritted, pulling my hand away from the wall. I didn't check, but I knew I left blood.

I could feel it dripping down my fingertips.

Some looked at that wall, the blood, but others didn't dare before going back to what they were doing. The wall could be their faces, and they weren't challenging me.

I panned back to LJ, the one who'd spoken, and with a wave, had him coming with me to the corner of the clubhouse. If we were going to talk about this, I didn't want any more ears in our direction. He came with me, and seeing us sectioning off, Knight and Jax immediately left their game of chess and came with. They'd been playing by the fireplace, watching over things while LJ and I talked. For the most part, it'd been business as usual at Windsor House, nothing funny, but we weren't taking any goddamn chances. We had no idea what *ears* were in here, all of us connected to uncles, cousins, and even fathers and grandfathers. We couldn't trust anyone, only ourselves at this point.

Hands propped, I waited for the boys to come over. We often chatted to ourselves, the perks of being from some of the original families of the Court. We didn't make the rules but we basically did. We *chose* what happened around here, who was in with us like LJ. He wasn't one of the OGs but if he was with us he was, our friend since kindergarten.

I paced. "What's Ramses' request?"

Too much silence, I looked up, handed a white handkerchief from Jax. I had no idea where he'd gotten a handkerchief, but I fucking took it.

My hand burned like hell.

I bound my bleeding knuckles, thankful for the gesture, but there still wasn't enough talking around here for my liking. If Ramses was putting in "requests" and shit, that wasn't good.

I saw that all over LJ's face, the one with the information. The dude looked like a college boy already with his university hoodie on. He'd already heard from and accepted the full ride offer from the top ten school he got into, which was well deserved. He worked hard, took care of his entire family since his dad up and left in middle school. The tall blond a tank, he braced his arms. "I'm not completely sure, but if I had to guess, entry into the Court. I've heard whispers about it."

"Whispers from *who*?" I growled.

LJ's sigh was heavy. "Some of the guys around here? The whispers started after Christmas Eve."

Christmas Eve... a hailstorm all around us, despite not having heard anything since that day. Ramses made threats that night, dark threats that if he weren't careful would get him in more trouble than he ever realized. He was delving into things that scared all of us enough to make us leave our homes, come here. I hadn't spent one night in my own bed since after we found out about Paige. That's when my life had changed.

That's when *all* our lives changed.

"He's going to get himself involved in some seriously messed-up shit," I said, the reality for all of us. We were all getting in deep, but that was on us. We had to, no other choice. I shook my head. "And if the Court council agrees to see him?"

"They'll review the request," Knight chimed in. The dude didn't say much, but when he did, we listened. He was more knowledgeable about the Court handbook, as his grandfather was on the council along with other senior members. He nodded dark hair. "And if they agree his argument is sound, there'll be a collective meeting."

The collective, i.e., us and every other goddamn member of the Court. Ramses' request would be put to a vote, and if it got that far, he'd win by a landslide. At the end of the day, Court was about power. It was about influence, and Ramses being the son of our fucking mayor only helped his case. They'd all want him on. If only for who he was regardless of the fact he'd denied the Court before.

"He's trying to pull something," I stated, facts. He had no interest in joining our members before Christmas Eve. He told us that. My eyebrows narrowed. "He's opening up a can of worms he doesn't want to fucking open up."

Because I'd *end* him if he got in my way. I'd have to. Like I said, we had all gotten in too goddamn deep. We were invested and we had to be. We owed that to a friend. *I* owed that.

I owed Paige Lindquist everything.

Ramses believed he'd scratched the surface of something on Christmas Eve, a surface that was not only dangerous for him but all of us. There was a reason we weren't staying in our homes anymore...

A devil in our house.

"It's not just that, Royal."

Jax faced me, looking worried most of the conversation. The guy didn't smile as much as he used to, jokes long gone. If any of us were kids before all this that happened with Paige, we weren't anymore. We were dealing with some real stuff here, having to be men if we were ready or not. Jax rubbed his buzzed head. "You know how you told me to watch him? Her?"

Her.

I nodded, knowing that well. I'd been on my guard about Ramses and his relationship with December, Paige's sister, already, but that got so much worse after his accusations at Christmas Eve. I wanted December watched, *necessary*, and Jax had stepped up to do that for me. "Yeah."

His jaw moved. "Well, he's been seeing a lot of her."

"Define *a lot*." I tabled my temper but only at the present.

Jax studied everything but me. "Enough to notice."

Enough to notice.

"He said he wasn't seeing her." A hand came down on my shoulder, LJ's. I didn't talk a lot about December, not with any of the guys. But I didn't think I really needed to. What December and I were or were not wasn't up for discussion and nobody else's business.

But that didn't mean the guys didn't know anything about it.

"Maybe that changed." Jax sat on the arm of a chair, his hands coming together. "Or maybe it didn't?"

But maybe it *did*, and since I couldn't guarantee that had nothing to do with what Ramses claimed over the holiday break, I had to assume the worst about his relationship with her. He was up to something, and whether he was seriously seeing her or not was possibly getting her involved in something I had no control over. I hadn't had control in a long time and God fucking help me if something happened to her too. It'd end me if something happened to her too.

I knew what I had to do, but that didn't mean I could stomach it. Getting my phone out, I brought Mira's number up, then gave the phone to LJ.

"Call Mira," I said, unable to look at him. Instead, I pushed off the wall, facing away. "Invite her over to the House and some other girls too. Make it a thing."

We'd done all this before... with her and the other girls, but it was different this time. This was post my meeting and relationship with December. For all intents and purposes, Mira was my girlfriend and had been since I put that silver necklace around her neck last fall. But even still, I hadn't touched her...

Not even a goddamn kiss.

Mira had her own agenda in this town and her own dirty work she was trying to do. She was using me for her own purposes, and since I was using her too, all was fair game. I'd kept her on a short but far-enough leash where I hadn't had to touch her. She enjoyed being with me, the influence of me, and since that kept her quiet about certain things, I put up with it. It also kept me close to a source I needed, her father.

I swallowed hard as bodies crowded behind me, a shake in my arms. I'd been getting panic attacks lately, even worse than before my mom and sister died. I'd been in a dark place then, but managed to be darker now. I couldn't help it with what I'd both seen and knew.

It'd prepare me for what I'd ultimately have to do.

We were playing with the big boys now, and anyone who I didn't want to be around for the fallout couldn't be. I had to protect December.

Even if I had to destroy her.

"Are you sure?" LJ asked me, and despite asking the question, he had his phone to his ear. He was ready for whatever I wanted to do. All the guys were. They knew the stakes here and weren't playing around. They knew my need to get December out of here regardless of what I'd told them about her and me, us. They'd help me run her out of this town.

They'd help me keep her out of the flames.

CHAPTER
TWO

Ramses

"Have the girls seen this yet?" Meaning one girl in particular.
I cringed at the display on my buddy's screen. December may
have kept whatever relationship she had with Prinze close to
the cuff, but no one, I repeat, no one wanted to see this
regardless of whatever relationship they had with someone.

Especially with what happened during Christmas Eve.

I didn't mean for things to come out the way they had,
and I obviously had been unaware she'd been in my dad's
study. But now that December knew what kind of stuff she
was dealing with, that made things a whole lot easier.
Nothing had changed since I left this town, absolutely
fucking nothing, and not only did that unsettle me, it pissed
me off it'd happened to her too. She'd gotten driven out of
this town, her sister *dead*, and once I found all that out, I
couldn't sit idle.

I wished I could have sat idle.

What was displayed on Luke's phone screen seriously
disturbed the fuck out of me, and I had no idea if this was just

how Prinze and his lot got their rocks off or if they were seriously just into some messed-up stuff. Whatever the case, December *didn't* need to see this. I waved Luke and the other guys at my locker to put the phone away, but by then, the girls had passed us in the hallway, casual traffic between classes. Birdie and crew shook their greetings, the basketball chicks always more like bros than actual girls. With Birdie there was Shakira, Kiki, and some of the other girls, and with the height of them, I'd been deceived December wasn't with them at first. She blended in with girls over a head of height on her, but not only was she there, she noticed the crowd over Luke's phone.

A dark head of hair eased out of the bunch, balled up and messy behind her head. She was the only one out of the lot of us who actually fit her academy uniform properly, the only one normal-sized with her petite shoulders and little body. She could easily be lost if one wasn't looking for her.

"What's going on?" she asked me, had to ask me first. It didn't help I was closest to Luke's phone screen. Looking guilty as hell, I hovered over it with my hands in my pockets.

I must have not been speaking quickly enough because she pushed into our circle, smelling like lilacs and other flowery stuff my housekeeper put in potpourri sacks around the house. I noticed December always had that distinct smell, smelling like home, and that really bothered me in the beginning.

It didn't so much now.

Nudging Luke, I took his phone, then handed it to December but only because I had to do so. I'd been caught right over it, the evidence there, and I pushed a hand behind my neck.

"The video was texted to him by like three people," I said, surprised I hadn't gotten it. At the announcement, the girls crowded around December too, studying the device, and that's when I looked up.

This thing was everywhere.

Literally people were on their phones all over the halls, hands over mouths and gasps in the air. It didn't take a rocket scientist to figure out what they were all looking at. Only so many things could elicit such a strong reaction, and the girls in our circle did the same. Many of them cringed, others murmuring, "Oh my God," but it was December I couldn't get a read on. She just stared at it, her dark eyes almost blank while she held the phone. She wasn't giving me anything to make a reaction off of.

She just watched the footage, completely silent, and worried by that, I eased in close to her.

"We don't know who all it is," I told her, honest. Upon watching the video, nothing but shadows could be made out. Shadows that moved and sometimes bounced. It was the sounds that brought the whole production into perspective, grunts of pleasure, moans, and needless to say, the imagination did the rest. This was an orgy before us, an orgy with multiple people, both guys and girls. Occasionally, the flash of a nipple would surface or even a dick shot, but with how dark it was in the room, it was impossible to determine who belonged to any of it. The way the footage was shot made everyone who participated completely anonymous and the only indicator Prinze, and obviously the rest of his lot, was involved was because Prinze himself was named. A girl had cried out his name.

One who mysteriously sounded like his current girlfriend, Mira.

She'd been in on this too, all of this disturbing as shit, and in my wildest, I honestly couldn't believe it. Stuff like this didn't happen in real life, not here and outside a frat house somewhere. This was a new low, dirty.

And was nothing but affecting people.

It affected one person in particular, and I watched the moment Prinze's name was moaned beneath the shadows. It was said repeatedly, the guy obviously getting a lot of action. December and her blank stare continued to absorb it all in, seemingly lost before me. The only reason the phone hadn't been taken from her by me was because someone beat me to it—Birdie snatched the device right from December's hands and thrust it at Luke. She smacked him over the head right after, she and the other girls calling it disgusting. I would have weighed in and agreed on that sentiment too, but was suddenly tugged by my uniform jacket.

"Come here," December said, just "Come here." I didn't get any more as she bowed out of the group and basketball girls continued to descend on the boys. There was a lot more head-smacking by Birdie in particular, and lost in all that, no one even noticed December and me pulling away from the scuffle.

She tugged me all the way down the hall and around a corner, Windsor Preparatory a madhouse with this video. Literally everyone was watching it as we passed them, watching *something*, and it was obvious what that something was. If Prinze was trying to make a statement, that was exactly what was happening. I wasn't really sure what that objective was, and maybe I was giving him too much credit. He was being a dick, and that showed by the way he obviously so didn't care about how his actions affected people.

And December was affected, her expression lost and almost pained as she leaned back against a set of empty lockers. No one used this wing of lockers at the school since they were older. She knew exactly where she was going, exactly where to go to be alone.

She was alone with me, my hands bracing my arms as I lounged back with her. Honestly, I had no idea how I hadn't made the connection between her and her sister when we initially met. She looked so much like Paige it was scary, same curve to her cheeks, full and pouty lips most girls over lined the hell with their lipstick just to achieve. Paige had a lot of girlfriends my freshman year, easy to see why, and though December was more quiet, they were like mirror images of each other. It only made what happened to her sister all the more chilling. Looking at December was like staring at a ghost.

She looked less and less alive in the passing days since Christmas Eve, all of this today even worse. I wanted to go back to Luke, take his phone and everyone else's just to make sure not a fraction of what I saw on December's face now ever returned. She didn't deserve it.

I dampened my lips. "You all right?" Again, I had no idea about her relationship with Prinze, but it was something. Besides this reaction now, Prinze had pretty much mutated into a fucking monster when I called him out on that. It was like a switch went off, the need for blood in his eyes. They obviously had something going on, at least at one time.

December's swallow was hard, her breath shallow when she folded her arms. "That was him."

Yes. Yes, that was Prinze, and yeah, he was a complete and utter dick for doing something like this full well knowing December would see it. It all enraged me, really wanting to know his end game, but since none of this was my business, this between him and her... My jaw moved. "Yeah, seems that way."

"And the other guys too." Her expression hardened. "Jax, Knight, LJ..."

"Probably, yeah." I didn't know a whole lot about them all, who they were now, I meant. But if they were in these halls and this place, they were acting just like the seniors I remembered when I went here. They were arrogant, self-centered, and threw their weight around. I supposed if I'd stayed that would have been me too. I was a piece of shit back then, and only arrogance would allow someone to do not just what those guys did, but post it somewhere for the world to see. This wasn't a mistake, a sex tape coming out. If they recorded it, they wanted people to see it. That much was true.

But did they realize the effects of such a thing, the effect on her, December? I continued to wait, December studying her shoes and, honestly, I wanted to call it right there. This was too much, too frickin' much to her, and maybe even cruel. Her sister had died for fuck's sake.

And you're using her.

I didn't know if that's what it was considered since December knew the truth about why I'd ultimately come back. She knew why I returned to Maywood Heights, this town and all this drama, and not only did she know, we were along for this ride together. We'd come up with a plan that Christmas Eve night, a plan we were already enacting, but this might all be too much for her. It might be too much for me to make her go through all this. We had to get inside the Court, and she'd been on board with that since holiday break ended.

That was before all this, before whatever all this with Prinze was. Since Christmas Eve, we'd little more than crossed each other's paths, an unsaid something between us, but we kept in each other's respective corners. I'd stayed, in his words, "on my side of the yard," but I wouldn't be for much longer. December and I were already putting things in motion here.

That was, if she was still on board.

I folded a hand over my eyes. "December…"

I was going to give her an out. If all of this was too much, it didn't matter what I wanted. I considered her a friend since I'd come back home, and friends didn't make their friends do things that caused them pain. I really wasn't the guy I'd been when I lived here anymore.

I dropped a hand. "If you want to call this, not go through with any of this, I understand—"

"Why wouldn't I?"

Surprised, I faced her, a determined look in her eyes I hadn't seen. Up until this point, she'd pretty much let the talking happen to her. She was with me, but she hadn't been "with me" if that made sense. True, she was all for what we'd planned to do, but where I'd been making those plans, she'd been sitting in the passenger's seat.

She didn't look that way now, her arms crossed when she stood up to me. She looked down the hallway. "We need to do this. Have you changed *your* mind?"

I hadn't, so I shook my head. I swallowed. "I just wanted to give you an out if you had."

Her tongue moved just a bit over her mouth, doing so clearly in thought. Even still, I stared for longer than I should have.

I looked away.

"I don't want an out," she said, causing me to find her eyes again. "I want revenge."

Revenge... so dark in ways again she hadn't sounded before. She'd been so broken that night on Christmas Eve by the information that had been delivered to her.

I knew because I had to pick up the pieces.

How long had we stayed in my father's study that night, not even talking to each other? We'd just been together, silent while the fire crackled in the corner. We sat so long I'd been numb when I'd gotten up, and by the end, I'd had to help her too. She was a shell when she'd left that room.

But maybe not now.

"Revenge," I said, and I got it. I wanted revenge too. My life had been destroyed by this place, Prinze, his Court, and what that Court meant to this town. It ruined lives, and it ruined me. My jaw clenched. "All right."

She faced me, her breaths even. "You hear from the council?"

She knew all about my proposal to them, no information concealed between us. She knew I put a bid in to be seen, to plead my case amongst the senior members of the Court. I nodded. "They agreed to meet with me, and it's all a go to do so. If they say I can pledge, there'll be a vote by what we call the Collective. Every member of the Court will be able to say if they're either for or against me joining. My odds are really good. I got lots of family in the Court."

My dad had been over the frickin' moon when I told him, his estranged son back and finally doing what was destined. It was things he'd destined for me, the mayor's son.

My eyes narrowed. "I'll be in the Court in no time."

Because that was the plan, we'd get inside the Court and do so together. I didn't have any power on the outside, could ask no questions to confirm what was going on behind the scenes. We needed to know more about what happened that night with her sister.

And the only way was to get inside the Court's house.

December was silent with this new information, silent but not vacant. She wasn't just a passenger on this ride anymore, something dark in her eyes, and that's something she probably had to have. She'd never survive this process, this town, if she didn't and the same was for me. In order to get into the Court, I'd have to do their haze, and it was a haze I'd have to do with a bunch of guys who didn't want me there. I'd made some of their lives hell when I'd been here, the epitome of a bully.

And I was sure they weren't going to let me forget it.

"And you'll get hazed," December said, pulling the words right out of my thoughts. "They'll do to you what they did to Paige."

It'd be what we *think* happened to Paige. Again, we still didn't know. "It could be anything, but I don't think it will be that. The senior members really didn't like that, and with everything that happened with your sister…" I pushed out a harsh breath. "They'd be too bold to try that again, and I'm sure whatever the guys end up doing, I'll be strong enough to handle it."

I'd have to be, if only for her. If I broke, she might break too, no option for retreat.

She faced me, nodding. "We're going to get them back, Ramses," she said, more of that darkness in her voice. "We're going to show this town who they really are."

CHAPTER
THREE

December

My feet slammed the track days later, whizzing past girl after girl in the academy's rec center. I didn't see people anymore, not in gym class like now or even in my other classes. They became a blur, an oblong deformity. They became an obstacle.

A hurdle came down the track.

I leaped over it without thought. I must have landed. What went up must come down.

Must come down…

Another hurdle, and I did the same as before, crossing into the path of another girl. I'd been quicker than her, quicker than everyone.

Gotta stay quick…

Breathing must have been optional. I didn't recall breath. I didn't recall thought. All memories and physical action were automatic. I breezed through life like I blew down this track, anything not to feel something. Eventually, a whistle pulled me out of the flow state, and it all hit me again. *Reality* hit. One had to breathe to survive, and life had to continue.

He had to pay.

The sickness I replaced with anger, physically swallowing it back as I sagged forward and attempted to catch my breath in my gym wear. The navy shorts and orange tee kept me cool under the recreation center lights, and the steady breaths kept me from falling. I latched on to them like a bat to a dark cave, the only thing I could do to keep my sanity. To my right, our gym teacher, Ms. Hollis, approached me, shaking her head with a smile as she wrote something down on a clipboard.

"Excellent time as always, Miss Lindquist," she proclaimed, stepping back when the rest of the class crossed her path. I'd been several seconds ahead of everyone, boys included. Ms. Hollis's smile widened. "I could have used you on the track team last fall."

Last fall...

I couldn't think.

You can't think.

I shut my eyes, some laughter and giggles saddling up beside me. I turned only to find red hair and a smug expression. Mira and her friends shared a gym class with me this semester, the only class we had together after winter break ended. Hands on their hips, they huffed between laughs, not as fast as me but that hadn't stopped them from giggling in my direction.

Mira cupped a freckled hand over her mouth, spinning a familiar silver necklace in her other hand. She always spun it, her lifeline apparently.

"Could have used you last fall," she parroted, mocking me to her friends but not loud enough for Ms. Hollis's to hear her. She never heard, going on to the other students and reporting their times to them.

Don't breathe. Don't feel.

Escaping the giggles, I physically escaped, heading over to the bleachers and grabbing a towel. I took the long way to the showers, the best way since no one else bothered taking the route. I was alone and gratefully when I finally made it into the locker room.

Recall went dormant again under chrome spigots, water hot enough to probably scorch the skin off most people but not me. I liked hot showers, my skin used to it after literally shower after shower this way. I did the same thing at home, well, at Rosanna's. I was still living there after break, and not only did I shower hot, I slept with noise, so much noise. I had Hershey, my chocolate Labrador puppy, in my bed, but I wore headphones when sleeping. I played rock music as loud as I could, maybe averaging an hour or two of sleep a night. It was the best I could do most nights and better than nothing. If I slept any other way, I had dreams, dreams about train tracks and my sister's screams.

I hadn't even been there the night she died and I heard her, the screams agonizing.

I chilled under hot water, her voice coming for me. She called out to me no matter what the time of day, and I couldn't stop the train. I couldn't help her.

At least not in the conventional sense.

My sister was gone, but I was not only here and alive, I wasn't without a means to help her. I may have lost my sister, but her truth didn't have to be. I had to report what was going on, what truly happened to her.

I had to bring Royal Prinze down.

He was so out of line with everything, that orgy he'd been a part of only consistent. It only showed he didn't give a fuck. Not about me or Paige. He was getting his itch scratched, and meanwhile, I was broken and my sister was dead. He didn't have a heart.

He didn't have a soul.

I turned under hot water, secure again in my stance. I was going to handle things the only way I knew how, and I had Ramses there to help me. He'd been burned too by the Court, and together, we were going to make waves. We had to.

Sounds told me I wasn't alone in the showers anymore, someone else choosing to use the same dirty old showers I chose. I usually came over here after gym because the uppity bitches at this school like to use the new ones.

I turned the thing off, grabbing my towel and wrapping it around me. I didn't see who'd joined me in the showers, and regardless, I didn't care. Instead, I made it to my locker, immediately going for my phone when I opened it. I'd been waiting for a text message.

Nothing.

I'd been waiting on a text from Ramses for over two days now, the kid basically ghosting me all weekend. He hadn't been without reason, though.

Where are you?

He'd had a meeting with that Court council after school the last day I saw him, something he told me in last period via text. I hadn't even gotten to see him before he left. He simply said, *Just notified they're meeting with me tonight. Here we go...*

I thought here we go indeed as I got dressed, trying my best not to freak out and worry. If something unusual went down he'd tell me something. We didn't keep secrets from each other.

We weren't like them.

Forcing myself to believe that, I unwrapped the towel from my body, but a buzz in my locker had me closing that towel right up. I immediately reached for my phone with thoughts of relief, but as it turned out that was fleeting. The text wasn't from Ramses, but Birdie.

I swiped.

Birdie: Hey! Want to hang out after school?

No. I didn't want to hang out after school. I wanted to know what the fuck was going on with Ramses. Gripping my hair, I shook that freak-out off and focused on my phone.

Me: Did you invite the guys and Ramses?

This was a possibility, and if she had heard from him, I could finally breathe again.

Birdie: I did.

Me: And?

Birdie: They're coming.

The sigh of relief started too early, another chime bringing me back down to the ground real friggin' quick.

Birdie: All but Ramses. He must still be sick or something. Didn't respond. You coming tho?

I didn't respond, putting both my phone and my head in my locker. My nerves were fucking shot, all this too much.

Don't feel. Don't feel.

If I did, they won, and I shut my eyes. Royal Prinze and his loyal band of cronies wouldn't rule my life. They could have everything in life, win everything, but they wouldn't rule me. I refused, and sucking all this shit up, I pulled my head out of my locker and got myself dressed. I didn't know where Ramses was, but by the end of the day, I was going to know something. I'd ask whoever I needed to ask to find out something. I had to, way too fucking worried for my own good.

I slid on my flats with more than a little aggression and only stopped a bit because I heard more giggles. *Her* giggles. It took all I had not to punch Mira in the face daily and for so many things. It angered me I still cared that she existed and even more that every time she spun that necklace around her neck, I wanted to strangle her with it. I shouldn't care, but for whatever reason, each and every time I saw her with it struck something in me.

I swallowed hard, putting on another shoe. I started to close my locker when the giggling sounded to inaudible levels.

"Oh my God. I totally can't believe you guys actually made a sex tape."

I paused, just standing there. It hadn't been Mira's voice but a friend.

"I know," Mira sighed. Another fucking giggle. "He hadn't touched me in weeks and then let his freak out."

The band of girly cackles sounded again, and I shook my head.

Hadn't touched her in weeks?

Unusual, I listened on, more of that bragging on Mira's end, but then another sigh.

"He's such a tease," she said. "He gives me all that, then totally leaves me hanging all weekend."

"Yeah. What was up with that?" one of her friends asked.

"Apparently, he was out all weekend making some pledge's life hell. Must have done a number on him because Royal's not even at school today."

My heart stopped, literally about to blast out of my chest.

"Hopefully, you can reach him today."

"Yeah, hopefully. You can't tease a girl like that and then—"

Screams, screams because I slammed my locker and scared the shit out of them. I hadn't cared, grabbing my stuff and leaving. I had my phone to my ear in two seconds, the final bell ending classes for the day right after. The halls immediately filled up, and I dodged people, trying to remain present on my call.

"Yo, this is Ramses—"

"Ramses, what's going on? Mira was saying all kinds of shit and—"

"You've missed me, but I'll be sure to get back to you soon. Also, leave me a text. Who checks their voicemails anymore?"

Groaning, I hung up, sending him a text. I asked him where the fuck he was and if I should worry. I asked him if I should tell someone… I don't know, anything about what we were doing. If he was starting to pledge, this may have come as a surprise to him. In fact, so surprising he might not have had time to tell me. Even still, whatever happened would have concluded after the weekend, right?

Dread befell me when I thought about the hazing process. I didn't know anything about the Court, absolutely nothing, but if Ramses started it and something went wrong, he might not be able to tell me anything. He could be hurt or worse, and my phone to my ear again, I blew up his. I left him another voicemail, rerouting to my locker to get on my coat and grab my book bag. In the next seconds, I had them on and then was sprinting out front.

"Good afternoon, Ms. Lindquist." My dad's driver, Hubert, was out front to meet me as per usual. I still was living at Rosanna's house, but Hubert was there to drive me to and from school. My dad insisted on him assisting me for whatever reason, and I only didn't fight it because I could use the ride.

Today, the help would be ill-placed, though. Hubert may take me wherever I wanted to go, but he'd most assuredly take those details directly back to my father. One thing about Ramses' plan was we weren't supposed to report anything we were doing to anyone. We didn't know who we could trust.

Even my own dad.

That man hadn't given me any reasons to trust him, and I wouldn't be starting now. I could use Hubert's help with a ride today, but it wouldn't be without a cost.

Faking a smile, I waved my hand. "Actually, Hubert, I'm hanging out with some friends tonight. I was going to get a ride with them."

The old man in a billed hat frowned. "Are you sure? I could take you."

I was damn sure, keeping that smile wide when I denied him again. Where I planned to go to work out this shit with Ramses would definitely shoot some questions out of my dad, and as of lately, he or my aunt Celeste hadn't butted their noses into my life. I think they were both scared to, scared I'd run again or do something crazy. Because of that, they'd both been leaving me alone, and I wasn't about to test the waters with that now.

I left Hubert at the doors of Windsor Prep after more assurances I didn't even believe. No, I wasn't sure I'd be okay, and I most definitely wasn't fine. My friend was out there most likely on a mission by himself, and I wasn't sure I had any power regarding the fallout. Ramses could be anywhere and doing anything.

Ramses may not have any time at all.

I kept myself together when I actually found my friends, the basketball girls crowded around Birdie Arnold's locker. Shakira and Kiki where there too, the girls all looking like the cover of *Shape* magazine, Olympian edition. They were gorgeous. They were tall, and even though I definitely didn't fit into their ranks with my lack of athletic ability, they chose to overlook that and hang out with me. I was grateful for that now, all the girls in the group brightening up when they saw me.

Birdie threw a long arm around me, her ponytail big, brown, and curly. "Hey, friend. You decided to come out with us after all?"

I didn't, and where I actually wanted to go made all the girls in the circle do a double take. They quite literally stared at each other a long time while I waited for them to get over the initial reaction. People were probably crazy to go out to Windsor House if they weren't Court, and I probably was. I had a bone to pick.

And I was going to make sure Royal Prinze fucking heard me.

CHAPTER
FOUR

Royal

A knock pounded on my door, and the bottle of bourbon left my fingers. It hit the carpet with a soft thud, and I groaned, pressing palms to my eyes.

What the fuck?

The knock reverberated through my room like thunder, and roaming through my sheets, I managed to find the bottle of whiskey I'd emptied last night. I tossed the motherfucker, the bottle hitting the door and shattering into a million pieces. The knocks stopped immediately, and throwing the sheets back over my head, I intended to get some fucking sleep.

Knock. Knock. Knock.

"What do you fucking want!" I roared, immediately regretting that. My hangover reached legendary levels at the sound, and I gripped my head, feeling like a stupid fuck for getting so drunk last night. Hell, it'd been more than one night. I day-drank all yesterday, the day before, and even early this morning.

I wanted to drink more, taking a pillow and pressing it

over my head. There was too much light in my room, my head spinning and throbbing.

And that blasted door.

Knocks hit again, softer this time.

"Royal?" started a voice, soft and meek. I didn't recognize it, but it sounded like a young dude on the other side. "Sorry to bother you, man, but—"

My thunderous steps roared through the room, and when I ripped the door open, a kid basically stared scared as shit at me. I'd surprised him, the kid stumbling back, and I pretty much had too on the way to the door. I was frankly fucking surprised I even made it over here.

I honed in. "Then why are you?"

He wrestled with his hands—Tyler, I think his name was? Anyway, he wore his Windsor Prep academy uniform, and it must have been later in the day than I believed. I either missed school or it was about to start. Either way, it didn't matter. I didn't care.

There was also two of the dude, the guy hazing in and out before my eyes. He swallowed. "There's a girl downstairs for you. Well, at the gates, and she's making a lot of noise about wanting to talk to you."

I rolled my eyes. "So?"

Girls asked for me all the time, nothing new.

He swallowed again. "I just thought you should know—"

I slammed the door in his face, told, so now he could go the fuck away. I returned to my bed, pulling the sheets back over my head.

Knock. Knock. Knock.

This kid seriously had a death wish, but as I didn't have the energy or stamina to deal with him, I buried into my bed like a vampire. I figured he'd eventually go away and would unless he wanted me to annihilate him.

"So you want me to tell her to go, then?" he asked. "She said her name's December…"

My eyes shot open, my stomach dropping. December?

My steps hit the wood panel floor again, and the kid looked in the midst of a sprint before I grabbed him.

"December?" I asked, getting him by his lapels. Why were there fucking three of this kid now? I shook him. "Did you say December?"

His throat jumped. "Yes, do you want me to tell her to leave?"

He should tell her to leave. She needed to fucking leave.

"Bring her to my room." I dropped him, my mind a blur when I slammed the door and immediately scanned my room. I had shit everywhere, glass everywhere, and I scraped it up enough to clear the door.

Why is she here?

Unable to breathe, I got the room in some kind of presentable state before thinking about myself. I wanted to shower. I needed to shower, but since I didn't have time, I decided to assault my closet instead. I found a shirt I thought may be clean, and after working it over my head, I had just enough time to splash some water from a water bottle in my face before another more lively knock came down on the door. Lively was actually an understatement.

I was surprised she didn't throw her fist through the wood.

"Royal!" Another slam and a smack this time like she bitch-slapped it. "Open this fucking door!"

She was angry at me, on fire, and though I'd given her more than one reason, I didn't know why today. Maybe she was ready to finally hand my ass to me, blow up on me and let me know she was done with me and, hopefully, this town too.

Prepared for that and what I'd do to push her more, I opened the door, her hand poised in my direction. Hair down and cheeks flushed, December wore a big-ass coat that made her look like marshmallow fluff. It was white and everything, completely unbecoming, and she drowned in it.

Then why did she still look fucking gorgeous?

She looked like a damn cherub with that flush in her cheeks, her skin a cream-colored porcelain like one of my sister's china-faced dolls. My dad never let the housekeepers put those away, there for his benefit as my sister hated those things. Even still, they were beautiful, ethereal.

Her hand falling, December stared at me too. I think, the two of us distracted by each other. I didn't look my best, hair all over the place and shirt untucked. My jeans I pulled out of the hamper, and she followed me all the way up from them to my face. She came here to raise some hell, and I'd *planned* to give it to her right back.

So why did I just want to grab her instead?

I shouldn't want that, not worthy of that. My sins were a mile long, and they'd only continue to grow. They had to in order to do what I needed to do.

"Okay," I said, shrugging and dismissive about it. I propped a shoulder against the doorframe. "I opened the fucking door, now what?"

I wanted to piss her off. I wanted to *push* her, and not only did I succeed, when her expression transformed, I got that when she physically pushed me inside my room. She slapped hands into my chest, little mitts that didn't even hurt.

"What do I want?" She pushed again, another baby slap. "What do I want?"

She raised her hands, shoving me again, and I only didn't fight back because I found I couldn't. I couldn't restrain her rage because I didn't want to. I deserved every bit of it, physically unable to hurt her anymore. It was ripping me apart every day, so I let her jostle me.

"Where is he?" She gripped my shirt. "Where?"

"Who?"

The question enraged her more, her boots crunching on

glass I missed picking up. She didn't even notice it with how on fire she was. She shook me. "Don't play with me—"

"I'm not," I said, taking one hand and then the other. Backing her up, I kicked my door closed, then pressed her against it. This was easy because she was so tiny.

It was also easy because she smelled like fucking heaven.

Her flowery smell physically made my mouth water, all of this a bad idea when I lifted her hands. Pinning her, I got her beneath me, drunk off her.

"Now who, princess?" I asked her, my sins growing more when I leaned in. My nose brushed her ear, and I closed my eyes. "Who are you talking about?"

I needed to let go of her because if I didn't, I knew what would happen. I'd let her in. I'd tell her everything if only to make the pain go away. It ripped me raw, worse and worse every day. Some days, I actually thought I'd buckle beneath it. She was the only thing that threatened my course of action, her and her damn flowers.

I breathed them in, wanting to sink inside her. I wanted to be part of her, and I wanted her to let me.

She did nothing at first, and I was scared of what she'd say next. I was scared she'd unravel me.

Instead, she told me to let go.

The words had been light but present, and when I pulled back, she had her eyes closed. All too quickly, she let out a breath, and when I let her go, I got back mine.

You're so fucking stupid.

There wasn't a world in which this girl and I could possibly be together. Too much had happened, and too much was still going to happen. She wasn't supposed to be here.

"What do you want?" I asked, gripping the chair at my desk. I closed my eyes. "Why are you here?"

Why was she haunting me? A ghost like one of my sister's china dolls. Her feet crunched more glass, and when I turned, she'd stared down at the floor. She noticed the glass, scraping through it, and eventually noticed the room too. It was in more than a disarray even with what I'd tried to do before she came in. I had stuff everywhere when things were normally tidy, and the amount of empty booze bottles that lined my dresser drawers and even my desk she'd definitely taken in. She started to look at the tower of shot glasses on the desk and the bottle of tequila I had beside it before I crossed my body in front of them both.

Her expression chilled. "Where is he, Royal?"

"I asked you who, princess," I said, turning around. Opening my desk, I slipped my hand inside. "I'm not a mind reader."

If looks could kill, I'd be dead where I stood when I passed a glance her way. She shot daggers at me, sinking her hands into her big ole coat.

"Your *girlfriend* was going on about how you made some pledge's life hell all weekend in gym class today," she said, her eyes to the floor again. She pushed out a breath before facing me. "So if you have Ramses—"

"Mallick?" Enraged now. *Livid*, I seethed. My hand in my desk, I pulled something out, gripping it. "What about him?"

Of course, she was here for him. The two of them besties, and I felt like an idiot again.

She's not here for you.

The reality of that forced me to consider all the acts I'd done, all the things I was *going to do* to make sure she put herself and this town in her rearview mirror. December didn't belong here and especially not right now. I thought I was protecting her.

I'd only screwed myself, doing things I didn't want to do that not only made me sick but were pointless. Touching other girls had been pointless. She was over me.

The vacuum suck of that was heavy, my insides cut worse than they should. I shouldn't care and maybe her lack of emotional tie would keep her away.

That's what you wanted.

I supposed the ends did justify the means after all. I closed my eyes.

"I want to know where he is," she said behind me. "He told me he was pledging to get into your Court."

I raised my head, my breaths harsh. "Did he?"

"Yes. So if you have him…"

I turned, gripping that object out of my desk. I kept it behind my back, running my hands over it. "What makes you think I have him?"

And what else did she *know*? What else had he told her about what he thought he knew? He wouldn't be that stupid. He wouldn't… hurt her with nothing but theories. He would possibly if he wanted to hurt all of us, hurt me. He may not know anything about my relationship with December, but he knew I was friends with her sister. I'd protect her at all costs.

An attack on her would be a hit against me.

It made me long to rewrite history and how I'd handled recent events. I'd made a judgment call, and maybe it'd been the wrong one, but when December approached me, eyes on me, I took those thoughts back again. I hadn't made the wrong choice.

And I knew just as well as her standing in this room.

She cared about Mallick, was friends with him, and though that drove me fucking crazy, that was the truth. The pair had a tie. They had a friendship or whatever.

She wet her lips. "Because you are the king of that group. You have *influence*, so you know everything that goes down. You tell me where my friend is or I'm calling the fucking cops."

She didn't know anything, and I knew that by the innocence of her accusations. She just wanted to know where Mallick was and needed my help to find him. I should be relieved by that.

My jaw clenching, I turned away, opening my hands and

pushing a red cloth onto my desk. It was a handkerchief, old and worn and something my friend told me to keep. She hadn't wanted it back after she'd given it to me to use.

My throat jumped. "Check the woods," I told December, facing back at her. "The woods by the school."

She simply stood there, stared at me, but in the end, not for long. She left my room, nothing but her scent in the air, and my head sagged forward. I'd made the right decision regarding Mallick.

The ultimate result of anything else would have gutted me.

I knew that for a fact, which was why I'd made the decision I had. After December left, I was alone in my room, but not for long.

LJ... Jax, Knight, and LJ opened my door. They didn't come in, though, just standing there.

"You told her where Mallick is?" Knight asked, obviously having heard our conversation in here. He may have even passed her in the hallway.

Putting Paige's handkerchief away, I nodded.

LJ frowned. "You know there'll be repercussions from that, from her being here? Half the house saw her."

"And heard you both." Jax came in, cringing. "Your voices traveled down the hallway. People know Court business was told."

It didn't matter what our brothers knew, at least the ones here. It just mattered what got back to other members, a certain member in particular, and I'd deal with that like I always did.

I'd basically had to my whole life.

CHAPTER
FIVE

December

The evening was cold, my breath in cloudy puffs as my boots crushed ice-lined leaves. The days had been warmer recently, but not warm enough. If Ramses was actually out here, some-where out here behind the back of the school, that was crazy.

If Ramses was out here, he could be dead.

My friends didn't even believe me when I told them, rushing back out to the car like a crazy person. I'd been talking a mile a minute, freaking out about the possibility of Ramses even being out behind the school. They hadn't gotten it until I told them he pledged for Court. I hadn't had a choice but to admit the truth.

I needed help searching.

I didn't know how long it'd take to find Ramses in the woods, but I definitely wasn't going without help. Along with the group in Birdie's car, we'd been able to recruit pretty much the whole female and male basketball teams. If someone wasn't out here looking, it was because we hadn't gotten a hold of them. Ramses had a lot of friends, and everyone wanted to help. Currently, his name traveled through increasingly dark woods, the day shifting into night. The girls and myself huddled for warmth, the boys searching in other parts of the woods. The girls stayed together while the boys searched in smaller groups.

"Ramses!" I called out his name, several more of the girls doing the same. In their coats, they called just as loud and with just as much urgency as myself. We had to move quickly.

It was getting so cold.

Winter had been forgiving since December, but still, this was the Midwest, temperatures temperamental. Especially as things got dark. Soon, it'd be completely nightfall. Shakira shook her head. "Are you sure this is where Royal said he was? It's too cold, December."

It was too cold, all of this crazy. Especially if Ramses was out here for more than a couple hours. What kind of challenge could they possibly have had him out here for even? Did he have to just stand there, wait for someone to come and get him? That seemed way too easy, and if a previous haze had to do with lying on train tracks, it was too easy.

The fear running rogue through my veins, I faced my friends. "We need to split up like the guys. Smaller search parties."

They nodded, myself somehow the leader of all this. They were looking to me for guidance, and I knew less about this school and these woods than they probably did. Even still, they took my advice, some with their flashlights triggered on their phones. It really was getting that dark, and after pointing in various directions, I led the girls to scan those areas. I had my own party, but in the end, started racing off by myself.

"December!"

My name was called as I charged forward, no time at all to

be going slow. I'd be okay and had to be way more than Ramses was currently.

What the hell is wrong with Royal?

Because this was dark, so dark. This was madness and if they really made Ramses stay out here to get that damn Court ring, they really were trying to kill him. Ramses said he could survive whatever they threw at him, but I was sure my sister thought that as well.

The whole thing made me sick, hard to even walk in the darkening woods. The only thing keeping me charging on was because I knew I might be the last thing keeping Ramses from a similar fate. He needed me like my sister didn't have that night.

"Ramses, please, if you're out there, say something!" My voice moved the trees, birds literally flying out of them and into the woods. In my ear, I heard similar calls, our friends searching for him too. I turned on my phone light the deeper I got into the woods, and waving it around, I caught an object before doubling back.

What the fuck?

My phone light caught three objects, people who scattered the moment the light hit them. The people had their faces covered, wearing black surgical masks over their faces like I'd seen in KPOP videos. Running off, two of them bounded away from the third in the center, and I raced that way, the other person sitting and slumped.

No way.

My light moved over a body sitting in a chair, literally hanging off it and slumped forward. They were naked down to their boxers and sneakers, shaking with a black bag over their head.

I dropped my phone.

"Ramses!" I ran like I'd never run before, faster than even in gym class and on stable ground. The body twitched at my sudden presence, long legs and lanky arms both bound at the wrists and ankles. Skin normally aglow with tan had turned pale, his body literally uncovered in the middle of the goddamn woods.

"Ramses," I cried, immediately going for the bag. They'd secured it with string but it wasn't tight. I pulled it off easily, and even though Ramses had twitched before, he wasn't moving now.

He sat there, eyes closed, and I didn't even know if he was breathing.

"Guys, help me!" I screamed, shaking him. I put my hands to his face. "Ramses? Ramses, look at me."

He said nothing, icicles literally on his eyelashes and curly hair. Ripping my glove off with my teeth, I checked for a pulse.

"'Zona?"

My heart beat with the pulse at his neck, his face shifting. His cheek touched my hand, so cold. He smiled a little. "You're so warm."

"Oh my God, Ramses." Shaking, I didn't move, letting him take my heat. Unzipping my coat, I braved the weather to put it around his bare body. He shivered inside it, and using my hands, I warmed him.

His grin widened. "Mmm. That's nice, and I have to say, you took long enough."

I'd hit him if I wasn't so scared for his life, and when our friends arrived, some of them actually screamed. I wasn't surprised. Ramses didn't look good.

He couldn't even raise his head.

He kept it down while he'd spoken to me, and I shouted for someone to call an ambulance.

"No, don't," Ramses urged, moving into my heat. I had my arms completely around him now, giving him all the heat I had. "Don't let them."

He'd whispered it all in my ear, my head shaking. "You're going to the hospital."

"No. I haven't been out here very long. Maybe an hour? The other guys left when they heard you coming."

I'd seen them leave, but he was crazy if he thought he wasn't going to see a doctor. He could have hypothermia or worse.

"Please, 'Zona," he edged. He pressed his cheek against mine, and suddenly, he was warm too. He was raw heat, fire, and even more when I slid my arms inside the coat and around his naked body. We were both in the puffer coat's heat, our own sauna created as his face rubbed mine. "Just get me home."

The urgency there I didn't want to listen to, but if he'd gone through all this to accomplish something and going to the hospital might undo that for some reason...

I held him tighter, telling our friends we just needed to get him home. They thought I was fucking crazy, and I did too.

And so was living in this town.

CHAPTER
SIX

Ramses

My friends were literally freaking the hell out. I was fine, and I told them that when I finally started to feel my toes. I really hadn't been out there for that long, and despite that, they all decided to stay at my house that night. They all stayed, even December, which gratefully I hadn't had to explain to my parents since they were out of town on business. They didn't keep up with much in my life, but a couple dozen guys and girls parking it at my house for an evening, yeah, they might have a little issue with that. My friends worked in shifts while I shivered under heating blankets and in front of space heaters. The girls had been in charge of food duty. I had soup and chicken broth literally coming out of my ears by the end of it. I couldn't sleep I'd been so full, and eventually, the majority of my friends bailed out about daybreak. They needed to get home and ready for school, and I needed to crash the hell in after a night slash weekend of freaking hell. The Court hadn't gone easy on me, and it wasn't expected. I needed to be a little uncomfortable to join their ranks, and truth be told, if they'd tried anything light on me, I would have fought for more. I had to make a statement.

I think I made it.

Nothing was sweeter than the look on Prinze's face when I not only rose to the challenge but literally did everything they said all weekend. The guy had made me his bitch, and I acted like I enjoyed every moment. I wasn't weak and showed no weaknesses. I went into those woods and put that bag on myself when it was all said and done. I sat there, not expecting the worse but ready for it. One would have had to pull me out of those woods before I walked out on my own.

I guess in the end that's how it turned out.

I think it was around mid-morning the next day I finally found myself coherent enough to talk to people again. Like I said, the friends had left around dawn, and they all checked in as they did. I'd been in and out of it then, but I recalled pounding a fist or two. The guys had given me props while the girls looked like they'd wanted to kill me. I'd scared them and even more so when I refused to go to the hospital.

I almost regretted that a little bit now as I stirred in my bed, sunlight a bit too much for the day. I folded hands over my eyes, rubbing the sleep out. My arms still a bit weak, I returned them both to my sides. I found warmth there.

I found December.

I shifted, then froze… December on my bed and a lot closer than I recalled her being last night. True, she'd been the one in and out the most, looking after me the most. I thought she'd read me the riot act like most of the girls had about trying to join Court, but not only had December held her opinions about my decisions, she'd helped me. She'd directed all the girls and even some of the guys last night, making sure they stayed out and gave me anything *I* asked for or needed. She'd listened to me.

She'd been a friend.

This friendship was why our current position was so

awkward now, the girl literally up on me, and with where my proximity to her had been, maybe something I hadn't fought in the night. I settled an arm around her slowly, December really that close. She lay on top of my sheets but she was with me.

I shifted, staring down at her. She was fully clothed, the only thing missing her coat, and I turned completely, just looking at her for a second. She slept soundly, looking like last night hadn't even happened with her little arms tucked in and her face on my pillow.

Don't do that. Don't…

I gave myself only a few moments before coming back to my goddamn senses. In the end, I put space between us, retreating over to my side of the bed. Before I lay back down, I grabbed the shrug my grandma made me one Christmas located at the foot of my bed. I made sure it was around December tight before grabbing my phone. I had a couple calls to make.

Things were going to change when we were both awake.

CHAPTER
SEVEN

December

Warmth radiated around me, undisturbed and subtle. It'd reminded me of a place I'd been in the middle of the woods, so much cold around me but there was one place where it wasn't. It was under my coat with Ramses when I'd been trying to get some heat into him. He'd scared the shit out of me.

The bastard.

I only couldn't yell at him because I'd been scared, and that fear I took into the night. Only when he was out of the worst of it did I finally get some sleep.

Poke.

Something touched my nose, something rubbery, and I opened my eyes to see messy brown hair, a grin, and a fucking pencil in Ramses Mallick's fingers.

He pulled it back. "It's morning, sleeping beauty. You can wake up now."

Morning...

I launched up, a blanket sliding off me. I didn't remember

putting that on, but maybe I had. In any sense, I was too busy freaking out to think about that. I fished around the bed for my phone, but when I pulled it out, I found no messages from Rosanna.

"Don't worry. I texted her you were staying at a friend's house," came beside me, Ramses when he sat up and dropped his pencil. He stretched long arms, that wingspan of his cutting across his entire king bed. His comforter had dropped to his lap, pooling in a heap at surprisingly chiseled hips. The guys had put him to bed basically the way we brought him in, all of us pretty frickin' frantic that night and Ramses definitely had made it to the gym a time or two. He had a subtle definition only made out by the golden skin he got from being a mixture of races between his dad and mom. I might have noticed all that he had going on a little more had I not feared for his life last night.

Still pissed about that, I scanned my phone to check out whatever text message exchange had been done between Rosanna and "me." There actually were a few freak-out texts on her end since my faux response Ramses sent wasn't received until early this morning. He told her I was fine and sorry I didn't check in. I was apparently up all night with Birdie studying and fell asleep. He actually managed to convince her to get me out of school for the day too, which was pretty nice. Seeing the time, we were pushing lunch now.

I lowered the phone. "Thanks." Ramses knew about my living situation, how I wasn't living with my dad. It'd come up a time or two in casual conversation, and I was happy it had now, since he got me off the hook.

Flashing another grin, Ramses took the next seconds to put a shirt on, one he'd found in his dresser drawers beside the bed. I honestly didn't think any of his nakedness at all would bother me. I'd seen more than enough last night, but for whatever reason, I definitely noticed when he no longer wasn't. Things felt a little easier, less awkward? Anyway, I was glad he did it.

He bunched the flannel at the sleeves. "No problem. The least I can do considering you kept me alive last night."

Remembering that, the anger flooded back. He was so nonchalant about that. I smacked him. "And what the hell was all that about? How long were you out there? What happened—"

"I told you an hour, 'Zona."

"Yeah, but what you didn't tell me was the details. You texted me you were having a meeting, Ramses. A goddamn meeting not that."

Seriousness lined a face normally laced with humor. He frowned. "That is how it started."

"So what happened?"

"They agreed to a vote between all the members, the Collective. The vote happened and the decision was obviously made. They allowed me to pledge, the conclusion of which you walked in on in the woods."

But it was so... fast. "Is it always that fast? The process?"

He clasped long fingers together, and when he frowned again, I assumed I was right about this being unusual.

"My dad was there," he said, looking at me. "Flew right in just for the meeting. He's on the council, but he was out of town, so I didn't think he'd be there. I have a feeling the quick vote was all him. It was all set up and everything, happened within *literally* hours after the council agreed to let it happen. Those who didn't show were allowed to vote via teleconference. A done deal. I got my request."

I frowned now. "So he wanted you to join?"

"Did he want me?" Sarcasm laced his laughter. He bunched curls. "He obviously made this whole thing happen, rushed it to hell. Let's just say after the council decided I got a big goddamn hug. His legacy continued."

What was with the fathers in this town? Were they seriously all as crazy as mine and Royal's? I shook my head. "And he didn't mind you getting hazed?"

"He didn't know about it." His hands came together again. "At least the details of it, but it is all a part of the process. He could assume that's what was going to happen next. After the vote, the good ole boys left, and the young guys came in, quickly taking me away."

"What did they make you do?" I cringed saying it. Mira said Royal and the others had tortured a pledge all weekend.

Ramses leaned back in his bed pants and flannel, way too nonchalant about this for my liking. "Really, you saw the worst of it. On Friday, they took me away blindfolded and used scare tactics to try and freak me out. Loud noises and flashing lights. Minor stuff. Anyway, they left me that way in a basement that night. And it was a heated basement before you ask, so it really wasn't that bad."

Even still, I cringed again, but Ramses only smiled.

"I was *fine*, a little hungry but fine. They fed me gruel, some crap that looked like oatmeal but definitely didn't taste like it. After meal times, I was forced to serve the guys their meals, then clean the entire Windsor House. It really wasn't a big deal and concluded out in the woods, which you saw."

"They could have killed you."

"They wouldn't. Honestly, they were about to take me in until they heard you and the search party. I heard them talking about it, 'Zona. They wanted to freak me out. They didn't want to kill me."

But they could have, and as far as I knew, they just might have had we not come.

"What do our friends know?" he asked, raising his knees under the sheets. "I mean, what do they think is going on?"

I'd had to dodge that bullet several times last night. I shook my head. "Next to nothing. Beyond thinking you're crazy, they just believe you're just going for Court again. They didn't ask why."

And maybe they didn't need a reason. They hadn't the first time. He was obviously legacy, so that was probably enough for them.

He nodded his head. "How did y'all even find me? I didn't reach out or anything."

"Royal," I said, making his eyes widen. "I put the pressure on, and gratefully, he told me."

I honestly didn't think he would. I mean, why would someone without a soul want to help me, but he had. Ramses sat unusually silent with this information, and when I pushed his knee, I got his focus back. "What's up? Why are you looking like that?"

He folded fingers into his curls. "Just wondering why he'd break code is all."

"Code?"

He shrugged. "I don't give a shit about it, but there's a code. Court information doesn't leave Court. If it does, there are consequences."

"What kind of consequences?"

He grinned again. "I've never been Court before, remember? No idea, but Prinze will hear it for that. You must have really put the heat on him."

Thinking about how he put the heat on me, I faced away, hating that part of the confrontation most of all. When he pinned me in his room, I hadn't stopped him.

At least not quick enough for my liking.

"So you're in now?" I asked.

"Almost. I just need to get my ring, and we're squared away and actually," he said struggling a bit when he threw legs over the side of the bed. He was still a little weak obviously, and when he tried to stand, falling back down, I launched off the bed.

"Ramses, what the fuck?" I grabbed him, making him lie back down. "What are you doing?"

"I gotta go pick up my ring," he said but all attempts at

movement had him laying his head back. He folded a hand over his eyes. "As soon as I can bear weight again."

This guy was seriously out of his mind. I pulled the blankets over him, and needless to say, he didn't fight me this time.

He grinned. "Thanks, Mama."

I shoved him. "You're not going anywhere, and where's your ring?"

"At the jewelry store," he said, sighing. "They sized me for it at the start of the weekend. Told me I could pick it up if I survived." He started to chuckle but stopped as he watched me leave the bed. "'Zona?"

Finding my coat on the floor, I put it on. "Do you need anything while I'm out? I'm going to go get your ring."

"Uh?" he started to get up again but stopped, his arms dropping like weights to the bed. "Don't do that. I'm going to get it."

"Hmm. Will that be before or after you pass out? Shut the fuck up. I'm going to get your ring. Now, do you need anything else while I'm out? I have the day off thanks to you, so might as well use it."

That logic had him eyeing me, but since he was so obviously in no state to argue, he pointed a finger to his dresser. "My wallet is on top. There's a silver card in there. Get it out."

I did, finding the card easily. It was metallic, a chrome finish, and actually had some weight to it.

Ramses sat up. "Show it to the guy at the jewelry counter, and he'll know you're legit. I called just this morning, and they said it was ready. You can borrow my car. The Benz is parked in the driveway."

I'd driven some really nice cars, but his Mercedes would be an even greater level. My sister's Range Rover ran some digits, but his Mercedes Benz was easily well, *well* over six figures. I'd be more intimidated by that if I didn't want to get this done. Ramses told me he didn't need anything else, and after pointing out his keys, he lay back down. I got my coat zipped up the rest of the way, then stopped at the door.

"Where am I going by chance?" I asked, tapping on my phone to prepare looking up directions. I was almost out of a phone last night too, thanks to him. I'd found it in the woods only after we found him.

Ramses put a towel over his eyes like a diva. We'd dampened a few for him last night. He burrowed into his bedding. "Prinze Jewelers. It's down on Main Street. Can't miss it unless you're an idiot."

He eyed me when he lifted the edge of the mask, and I flipped him off. I started to ask him about the name of the place before I left but I wasn't an idiot. Royal's family obviously was in more than the veterinarian business.

Hell, it wouldn't surprise me if they owned the damn town.

CHAPTER
EIGHT

December

Ramses' car was a stick shift, and I killed it about seven times on the way to downtown. The last time I'd been behind the wheel of a stick shift was literally when I learned to drive on my aunt's old Cutlass.

I managed to get the thing in a parking spot, and after hitting the key fob a few times, I got it locked too. The issue was the car kept unlocking itself every time I got the fob anywhere remotely close to the door. I'd call the thing a piece of shit except for the fact that I was mad at it for being smarter than clearly I was.

Huffing, I got myself out of the street and up to the jewelry store, which stood alone between a couple mini malls. It was like Prinze Jewelers was its own display, the shops around a fair distance away. Glass windows displayed shining jewels, and when I opened the door, a *ping* chimed my arrival. I got the attention of about three people, all staff, and the one in the center holding up a diamond necklace the

Queen of England herself might faint for looked at me as well. This place was ritzy. This place was quiet, and I stood out like trash inside it. Mostly because everyone else wasn't under the age of thirty, nor were they wearing any coats like it wasn't cold outside.

"Can I help you, miss?" Mr. Holding-the-Queen's-Jewels immediately asked me. I'd barely had time to set a foot inside the place before he was handing the necklace off to an associate and approaching me. "Are you looking for someone?"

I noticed real quick how he didn't ask me if I was looking for *something*. In this town with all these richie rich kids, I definitely could have been here to spend mommy and daddy's money. Since I wasn't, I gave the guy the benefit of the doubt. I waltzed right up to him, flashing Ramses' card.

"I'm here to pick up something for Ramses Mallick," I exclaimed, more than a few eyes on me. I suddenly felt like a girl Friday retrieving something for my boss. I faced the guy in a suit. "A ring?"

Taking the card from me, the man stepped away and slid back behind the corner. Following him, I watched as he ran the card on some device.

His eyes widened. "There appears to be a mistake here. This is Mr. Mallick's card, but you're not Mr. Mallick."

What gave it away? I rolled my eyes. "I know. He sent me."

He eyed me, pursing his thin lips a little before placing the chrome card on the counter. "It's not customary to give out other customers' merchandise. Even with their buyer's card."

"I *told you* he sent me. You can call him, and he'll tell you."

He smiled a little. "Even still. It's not customary."

Completely over this, I pulled out my phone. I came all the way out here, and I wasn't leaving without the damn ring.

"What up? You get the ring?" Ramses asked, chewing on

something. It was a pretty loud something and almost sounded like popcorn.

Well, he must be feeling better.

I rolled my eyes again. "Yeah, so can you get this guy at the counter to give me your ring? He's handling me and won't let me get it without you."

"Ah. Is it Benjamin?"

I eyed the guy behind the counter, his look curious as he watched me on the phone. The man had no nametag, but he looked like a Benjamin if I'd ever seen one. I explained what he looked like to Ramses and heard a smile in his voice when he responded.

"Give me to him," he said in my ear, more of that crunching into the receiver, and I did, handing the phone over to "Benjamin." From over the counter, I heard a lot of "yes, sir" and "no, sir." Basically, there was a lot of kissing ass, and at the end of the call, Mr. Benjamin looked like he sucked a lemon.

Benjamin lowered his head. "I will have the piece for you in moments, and I apologize for the inconvenience, Ms. Lindquist."

So I was Ms. Lindquist now? Feeling a little smug about that, I thanked him before putting the phone up to my ear. "Thanks."

"No problem, 'Zona. See you when you get back. Call me if Benjamin gives you any more lip."

"Aye, aye, Captain."

Chuckling, he told me he'd see me later again, and after I hung up the phone, Benjamin returned with a black bag with a silver bow on the front. Out of it, he pulled a black box, presenting me a ring.

It was a Court ring all right, gorilla mouth and everything. Up until this moment, this all hadn't really felt real but here was that reality right in front of me.

We really were doing this.

Once that ring was on Ramses' finger, he was Court officially.

"I take it the piece is to your liking?" Benjamin stated, and after I nodded, he wrapped it up and returned it to the bag. He slid it over to me, swiping Ramses' silver card right after. He started to give it back to me, but something on the screen gave him pause.

He held up a hand. "It seems Mr. Mallick has one more piece of merchandise. If you'd excuse me for a moment. It requires special handling."

After handing me the card, he backed away, and I got my phone out again, prepared to give another call if this guy was trying to pull something. Spinning around, I decided to use the wait to look inside the cases, and look I did. There was easily enough precious metals in this place to purchase a town and maybe even had. Royal was clearly influential at school and why not his family the same? That all had to come from somewhere. I also remembered Birdie saying he and some of the guys had come from a few of the first families who founded the Court. He came from riches obviously.

"Benjamin tells me you're here to pick up something from our vault for Ramses Mallick."

I stared up from a jewelry case, my eyes widening at the man in the pinstripe suit before me. I'd only seen him twice, but both times he'd been cruel.

He'd hit his son the last time.

He'd done so right in front of me. Though he hadn't known I was there at first. I wondered if he'd even resist *knowing* I was there. Royal's dad hit him with so much force that day, enough to say he'd done it more than once.

I swallowed as the man came around the counter, came toward me, and he really did look like Royal, older but from the same gene pool nonetheless. Frankly, his dad looked like a slightly older Hemsworth if one of the brothers just so happened to be a dick.

My lips parted. "I just came for..."

"Access to our vault, which only I have access to." Mr. Prinze put his hands together, staring down at me. "The client has asked for care for this particular piece of merchandise. Care, which requires only handling by the president. It was a good thing I was here today. I was just heading out to my office at the bank."

Dear God, did he own the town's banks too? And hell, did he work with my dad? I had no specifics about what my dad did, but I knew his job required work at the bank. The man very well could be my dad's boss.

Well, that explains why Royal got anything he wants in Dad's house.

Dad had been hella submissive the one time I'd brought Royal over. At the time, Royal had claimed my dad simply didn't have a problem with him. Maybe he couldn't have a problem, too scared to.

I gripped Ramses' bag, and for a hot second, I thought about saying I was good. No way did I want to be anywhere near a guy who hit his kid, but stepping back may show him his power over me, which was the opposite of what Ramses and I planned to achieve. He needed to know I didn't feel threatened.

I lowered the bag to the side. "I appreciate the help, thank you."

His eyes twitched a little like he was surprised I decided to let him help me, and why not? The last time he'd seen me, he'd basically thrown me out of Windsor House. He'd had no reason, of course, and at the time, I'd believed it had to do with whatever vendetta he had against Royal.

Without words, Mr. Prinze waved a hand forward, allowing me to go first. I did, but did look back. I noticed rather quickly Benjamin decided to stay up front with the rest of the customers.

Bastard leaves when I need him.

I would have liked to have that buffer, but since I clearly wasn't going to get it, I went to the elevator with Mr. Prinze. He pushed a card inside once the metal doors closed, and a light flicked on to the lowest button. We were going to the lower levels.

Brilliant.

I could basically hear my heart beating in my ears, standing there and pretending I was okay. I had to pretend. I had to be brave.

You're okay.

The doors opened up and I only breathed when Mr. Prinze stepped out of it. I followed him, the walls lined with little boxes with key holes. Out of his pocket, Mr. Prinze took a key and opened one that said *1451*. Behind that number was a thumbprint pad, and after pressing his thumb down on the plate, a little door popped open. Inside, he pulled out a red box, thick but slender. It also had a key hole, gold around the mouth.

He presented the box to me without the key. "I didn't know you were friends with Ramses Mallick. You must be very close for him to allow you to pick up such value for him."

I took the box, a little weight in my hands. "No key?" I asked, deliberately ignoring what he said. Who I was friends with was no more his business than his own son's.

His mouth righted a bit, a quaint smile on his face before closing both the thumbprint and key lock door. He returned the key to his pocket. "No key. You have everything you need."

I nodded, sliding the red box into the bag. Mr. Prinze, on the other hand, put his hands behind his back.

"How you look so much like your sister," he said, his smile rising just a bit higher. "I hope you're staying out of trouble. My son has a way of corrupting people."

I was sure, if that was the case, he'd only learned that from him, his statement completely bold.

As well as hurtful.

What happened to my sister was more than fresh, but not only did I not let what he said affect me, I stood tall. "I thank you for your help again." It took all I had in me to say that.

The alternative was punching him in his goddamn face.

CHAPTER
NINE

December

I ran into interception after returning Ramses' car to the driveway, an interception that not only had my eyes widening but definitely gave pause to the guys I ran into. Three mini mountains came out of Ramses' front door, all wearing coats and looking amped the hell up upon crossing the threshold. In the front was LJ, his blond locks pushed up into a man bun at the top of his head. He apparently had an undercut beneath all that hair, the back shaven, and seeing me, he pushed out a hand and halted the other two. The other two were Knight and Jax, Royal's other two henchman.

Knight came forward. "What are you doing here?"

"I could ask you guys the same. Did you do something to Ramses?" I stalked up the steps toward the door, and breaking away from LJ, Knight stalked down, cutting me off. About probably two hundred pounds of thick and sizable male stood in front of me.

Knight snorted. "Did we do something to him? You gotta be joking."

"I'm not." I shoved him for good measure, and a hand crossed in front of us, LJ. He physically pulled us apart when he grabbed Knight by his puffer coat, tugging him away and making him walk down the Mallick household's grand steps. LJ followed after him after that, shaking his head at me.

I stood the high ground, watching them go. When Jax started to move that way too, I frowned at him. "You guys have some nerve coming here. After what you did to him, what *Royal* had all you guys do to him? You have some nerve."

I wanted to say more, so obviously having the floor here. Even Knight and LJ had stopped at the bottom of the steps. Jax crossed in front of me, though, and this time, he shook his head.

"If only you knew what the hell you were talking about, Lindquist," he said, frowning too. "Maybe if you did, you'd—"

"Jax?" LJ cut a hand across his neck, immediately silencing Jax. The blond waved him to come on, and despite doing so, Jax continued to stare at me.

Jax tipped his chin. "Maybe if you did, you wouldn't be so hard on him."

My brow twitched up at that, but even still, I wasn't backing down. In any case, the boys left after that, and I was too busy running inside to make sure they hadn't killed Ramses to read into anything he'd said. The first place I headed was up to his room, and when I found him sitting on his bed in front of his big-ass TV, I allowed my first breaths of relief. He was completely fine, sitting on his bed playing video games of all things. He was still in his bedclothes, aggressively fighting off some orcs or some shit on the screen, and seeing me, he shot me a look.

"What's with that face?" he asked, his attention back on the screen. He shot more orcs. "You look like you're about to kill someone. You get the ring?"

Dangling the bag, I showed him I had, and going over to his bed, I threw a pillow at him to make him drop the controller.

"I thought you might be dead, idiot, and yeah, I got the ring," I said, putting the bag on the bed. I took off my coat. "I ran into Knight, LJ, and Jax at the door. Thought they might have killed you."

With as skilled as he apparently was, Ramses not only didn't drop the controller but leveled up when he threw a fist into the air. Moving onto the next adventure on the screen, he got back into it. "Why would you think that?"

I rolled my eyes, tossing my jacket before taking a corner of the bed. "I don't know, because they almost did like a day ago."

He chuckled. "That was before. But now, things are different." He jutted a chin toward the bed, and by his feet were a couple of keys. He grinned. "Keys to Windsor House. Can you believe that?"

I didn't, picking them up. "They gave these to you?"

"Yep. One to the main doors, the clubhouse—sorry, that part's just for guys—as well as an access code into the whole facility." He put a finger up to his head for that part. "All in here. I guess I'm in, and not only that, they wanted to make sure I was okay. I guess you guys scared the shit out of them by pulling me out of the woods the way you did. They were just trying to see what happened to me."

Wild.

I threw hands through my hair. "Okay."

"Just okay?" Letting his character die, he put the controller down. He raised his long legs. "'Zona, this is exactly what we wanted. Their trust?" He shook my leg. "With them out of the way, we can go into Windsor House and ask as many questions as we want. This is a good thing."

Yeah, I guess so, and I watched as Ramses reached over and slid a hand into the bag.

"With this," he paused, opening and unleashing that shine of his big-ass ring. He pulled it out, sliding the chrome over a knuckle. "We literally have the keys to the castle."

"And that?" I asked, the red box peeking out of the top of the jewelry bag. "Something for your mom or something? I hope so. I had to talk to Royal's dad to get it."

"Really?" he asked, pulling that red box out. Without talking to me more about it, he opened his dresser drawer and slid it inside. "Surprised he left the bank for that."

"He was already there, and he owns the bank?"

Ramses' nod was subtle, but inside I said, *Jesus.* This was really what we were looking at here, people like that and with that kind of influence. I raised my legs, hugging them.

"What's up?" Ramses asked me, pulling in. "You don't look happy."

I should be, but I'd be lying if I said I wasn't intimidated. If I wasn't *scared* to find out the truth.

I mean, look what happened to my sister.

If it was a haze gone wrong and people surrounding that haze got the authorities to keep silent about it, what could we do? "You really think we can do this? That people will listen to us?"

"They will." Ramses nudged me with a shoulder. "I may not have much stake left in this town, but I am still the mayor's son. We can do this, but we need information before we can do anything."

"So that's what we're going to do?"

"That and a couple other things. This is going to be a process, but if you're game, I think we can really pull this off."

I was willing to do anything, do what I had to do to make sure whatever we needed happened. "What's next?"

Dropping long arms over his legs, Ramses faced me. "What's next actually starts tonight, and needless to say, you're definitely not going to like it."

CHAPTER
TEN

December

I got what Ramses was trying to say. For this next leg, things probably should appear to be normal in my life...

But seriously, what the fuck?

He wanted me to move back home, go home to my dad's house and under my dad's rule. He said doing so would give the guise of stability in my life. If I looked like I made amends with my father, wasn't making waves, no waves would ultimately crash around me. I'd just be a normal girl going to school. I *had healed* and moved on with my life.

Frankly, it'd been no different than what I'd been doing since holiday break ended. The only difference was, me still living at Rosanna's did give the appearance that there were still broken pieces in my life. It showed I was still at odds with my father, and if I couldn't get past that, I definitely wasn't okay.

I closed my eyes.

Rosanna had been simply overjoyed, of course, when I told her. She'd been home when I got in last night and had been so happy, in fact, that she called my dad right in front of me. He actually asked to speak to me, probably wanting to make sure I wasn't outside my mind, but since I wasn't certain of that, I avoided the call completely. I'd retreated to my room instead, packing. A text from my aunt Celeste came in after that. My dad must have called her, and she also wanted to confirm I was going home. After a lifetime of battling each other, they were apparently on the same side, and after I told her I was planning to go back, I suddenly had a ride home. My father's driver, Hubert, came over to Rosanna's within the hour.

Next thing I knew, I was home.

The place had felt so foreign when I arrived, empty. My dad gratefully hadn't gotten in yet, and after getting myself and Hershey settled back in my old bedroom, I pulled sheets over my head. I couldn't face it all. Not yet.

But then came morning.

It came with the reality of the day, and I had to force myself to move. This was life now, my new reality. I went on with the motions, hurrying quickly. I wanted to avoid my dad, but as soon as I heard movement around the house beneath my floor, I knew that wasn't happening. Dad had always been an early riser.

Fucking brilliant.

I wouldn't be able to avoid him today, that I knew. In any case, it was probably good to get the initial confrontation out of the way. I could say hi to him and do my best pretending.

Honk. Honk.

Hearing the short taps of a horn, I pushed back curtains, a Mercedes Benz in the driveway. Inside sat a boy, and when he caught me peering from the second floor, Ramses tossed a hand out the window. He appeared alive and well, grinning at me from behind a windshield. He told me he'd come to pick me up, and we'd go over a few things before classes started.

I gave him a quick wave before edging back in front of the mirror where I'd been. I looked like myself, orange and navy blue academy skirt on and tie nice and tight. I had even ironed my jacket.

But what illusions a mirror could give.

I wasn't myself anymore. I was different and had to be in order to even step out of this bedroom. Ready enough for it, I reached down to get my book bag.

A wayward traveler fought me back.

Hershey's big ole butt was trying to climb into the bag like she could still fit inside it, and talk about a girl happy to be home. My chocolate Labrador drifted right off to sleep the moment I placed her and her dog bed in my old bedroom. She hadn't even wanted to sleep with me like she did at Rosanna's, this place familiar to her.

I pulled her out, putting her down. "You can't go with me, even though I want you to."

She gave me her silly little grin, and after petting her, I started to lift the bag again, but she fought me. Jumping on it, she dove face-first inside, and she didn't come out empty-mouthed. The tie of a bow between her teeth, she tugged, unraveling it.

"Hershey," I scolded, and she did give it to me, but I froze at the sight of what the ribbon had been secured to. I had shoved so many things into my bags last night, and my book bag must have gotten some stuff too.

Taking a moment to breathe, I opened the bag to find a present given to me during Christmas break. I believed it to be from my father, the reason I'd instantly thrown it away. Only later did I find out the truth.

It was from my sister.

Well, it wasn't from her per se, but a friend who said it once belonged to Paige. I ran into my sister's counselor, Lena, at the Christmas party Ramses' family threw every year. She told me she sent the present over via my dad, and I panicked because I'd initially thrown it away. I'd ended up rescuing it from the trash that night, but even still, I had yet to open it. I think I hadn't been ready at the time, and with all I'd found out that night, I knew I hadn't been.

I sat cross-legged with it now, the package in my hand. Without thought, I ripped it open like a Band-Aid, quick to reduce pain. The floor quickly was covered in wrapping paper, and lifting the lid of a box, I discovered the bounty inside. A journal.

My sister's journal.

I ran my hand over a moleskin surface, the thing so nice and precious. Lena told me Paige wrote in it when she'd seen her as a freshman.

Breathing, I lifted the cover quick too, fearing I'd lose my nerve. I thought, upon seeing the insides, I might want to cry. These would be my sister's last words to both me and the world.

So why was I smiling?

Images filled my vision, gorgeous images of cartoons of all things, Japanese anime-like with big eyes and cute expressions.

Eyes...

There were many eyes, and some of them weren't even on faces. She had a fascination with them apparently, sad eyes, happy eyes, and all of them expression-filled. She had a lot of emotions here, and I realized that's how she displayed them.

Hershey crawled into my lap, still small enough to do that. Together, we studied these eyes until more honking outside broke me out of the trance.

I closed the notebook, extremely grateful for the gift. Lena, when she'd given the package to me, expressed I should see her sometime, but not just for counseling.

Maybe I will.

It'd be nice to see a friend outside of the crazy of Royal and this town. My sister had other allies, and it wouldn't hurt to see them as well. Getting myself together, I slid the note-book into my bag. I put Hershey in her kennel, then headed downstairs. The kennel was a new thing for Hershey, but only temporary until Rosanna came in for a shift at my dad's house. I'd bought the thing before I came over last night so Hershey wouldn't tear up the house while I was at school. I didn't need any more potential stress from my father.

My feet touched the stairs, and as I descended, I thought better of grabbing a quick breakfast. Dad probably wouldn't have anything anyway I could possibly eat since I was vegan. It'd been a "thing" before, so I rerouted to leave.

"December?"

My heart in my throat, my hand froze on the knob to the house. I turned to find my dad coming into the foyer from the living room.

And he didn't look like himself. Truth be told, I hadn't seen him since before Christmas, but he hadn't looked like this. Hair, dark like mine, was disheveled, and he had a dark-ness under his eyes like he hadn't slept properly in a while. His cheeks had even hallowed a little.

Had he been eating?

He was dressed for a day at work, sans the jacket, but he didn't look like he should work. He looked like he should sleep.

Not allowing myself to care, my hand left the doorknob, and I forced myself to look at him head on if only for appear-ances. I'd been told in the past we could have been clones. Well, except for the whole gender thing. My hair was obvi-ously longer, but we had the same long noses and fair features. Though, my cheeks were fuller at the present.

What happened to him?

Something happened, but whatever the case, I didn't care. I stopped caring about a lot of things. Especially the guy who hadn't given a shit about me *or* my sister. He told me that with everything he did, better to throw money at us than actually care for us growing up. I adjusted my book bag. "When did you get in?"

Basically making conversation, I waited for it.

Dad eased his hands into his pockets. "Late last night. I was away on business."

Always working, better at making money than being anything else, a parent amongst that list.

Nodding, I glanced at the door upon another honk, and Dad did too.

"Who's that?" he asked as I turned the doorknob.

Light spilled into the house.

"Ramses Mallick," I said, waiting for his opinion about that. He seemed to always have that. "Mayor Mallick's kid? We're friends, been hanging out."

Dad acknowledged that, his head bobbing once. "That's good. That's nice that... well, that you're hanging out with him."

Not Royal Prinze's biggest fan after all, and with what I assumed about him working with Royal's dad, that didn't surprise me. I wanted to ask him about that, but at the present, I definitely didn't care enough.

Instead, I grabbed my coat off the coat rack, then pushed myself out the door.

"Happy to have you back," Dad said, giving me pause. When I faced him, he smiled a little. "And have a good day at school."

He said that my first day of school, things so different now. We'd gone from no trust, to a little trust, to this.

I guess it was what it was.

CHAPTER
ELEVEN

December

Ramses kept the engine running of his Benz after he parked at school, the ultra-sleek ride I was finally taking notice of now that I wasn't killing it. It definitely stood the hell out and even in this parking lot with the wave of Audis, Beamers, and Range Rovers. He also drove a Mercedes when we lived in Arizona, but as I too had been inside that one, I noticed this one was slightly different, nicer even. Noticing me playing with all the various dials and knickknacks, Ramses chuckled.

"A gift from my pap," he said, doing a weird Southern accent with it. He really was himself again. Dressed to the nines, he had himself pressed and polished, his orange and navy uniform tie, dare I say, making him look very handsome behind his black wool coat. And did I mention he put some product in his hair? He actually managed to tame those normally wild curls of his. I decided to mess with them, and he grabbed my hands.

"A gift from your pap, huh?" I jostled, leaving him alone

when he whined like a baby about all the time he took on his hair. He really had, and it did look good.

He flipped out his lapels. "Yes, and he's very proud of the son who finally got on board with his legacy." He put a hand on the dash. "A peace offering."

Well, it was a hell of one. That was for sure. With this thing, I could pay a full four years of college easily. I smoothed my hand over the chrome finish for a second, and only stopped when I realized Ramses was watching me. He sat in silence, thoughts behind his eyes, and reality hit. All jokes should probably be gone right about now. He wanted to meet for a reason this morning, his first day not only back but as an official member of Court. Today would mean something.

"So what's the plan?" I asked, ready for it. I mean, I moved back home after all, didn't I?

"This morning go okay?" he questioned, asking about it. He grabbed his book bag from behind the seat, sliding mine over too since it was back there. "Nothing crazy with your dad?"

It maybe could have been if I allowed him to get his hooks in. I shrugged. "He's fine. We'll be fine."

He nodded, almost looking a little relieved by that, and maybe he was. I didn't let on about the issues my father and I had, but it wasn't a mystery. Ramses was probably happy the transition hadn't been as bad as it could have been for me.

He chewed the inside of his cheek. "Well, that's good. As far as the plan, let's meet at my car after school. Put to use those Windsor House keys? We can keep things casual, but we should probably start making some appearances. The more people we interact with, the more we can determine who we can get information out of it."

This was a good idea but would be different from the few times I'd been to the house. The first couple I'd been dragged and definitely not by my own terms, and the last I'd been so angry. I was angry now, but at least this time, I had some control. I would be going there with my own objectives.

And this time, I wouldn't be intimidated.

Seriously, each and every time I'd allowed the likes of Royal Prinze and crew to get into my head. I'd allowed *Royal* to get in my head, but this time I was in charge.

"Okay," I said, more confidence in my voice than I probably had. It was time to start the show and be the boss I knew I could be. I had to be for my sister, her drawings in my bag for strength. I'd take her with me today and everywhere I could, a reminder of what I was doing and who I was fighting for. I'd share her story. I'd *get revenge*, and I'd do it any way I knew how.

Ramses was doing that thing again, staring at me, and when I asked him about it, he mussed his own curls. He spun those long fingers in his hair and everything.

"There's something else too," he said, doing more of that cheek-chewing thing. "And it's completely optional, but I think it'll be our best chance at going at this undetected. Actually, it'll make us completely invisible if we do it right."

He was holding his bag, almost rocking with it.

He played with his hair again. "Again, let me emphasize this is optional—"

"Dear God, what is it, Arizona?" Though this was his name for me, I called him that too. That was our thing, a shared place we had between us. It connected us in ways in those early days I didn't think either of us would anticipate. It linked us much like these moments now. This kid and I had a shared trauma because of this town, this boy and I.

That very boy finally got his shit together and opened his bag, reaching in to bring out something I'd seen before. It was that red box I'd picked up from the jewelry store, the one with the missing key.

It seemed Ramses had the key all along when he pulled out his wallet. It'd been inside there, falling into his palm when he shook the wallet a little. The thing was so tiny, and he handed it out to me.

"I had the jewelers restore it," he said, clearing his throat a little. "The box was my grandmother's."

My eyes widening, I took the key when he guided his palm toward me. He wanted me to take it, and I did.

He passed the box second. "Again, this is optional. Just go along with me for a second here."

If this kid wouldn't shut up for a second and let me see what this all was about. I nudged him before putting the key inside the pretty box. Opening it up, I propped the lid open, and I did have to sit back against the seat.

The piece was beautiful, a silver necklace with a circle shape. It was also familiar, and staring at it, my lips parted.

"May I?" came before me, Ramses when he slid the gorgeous necklace out of the box. He held it up. "Do you know what this is?"

I did know what it was, resentful of it each and every time a certain redhead flashed it in my face. She did so as a trophy, bragging about what it was and what it meant. This was a Court-kept necklace, and every girl who wore one of those was "Court kept." The necklaces meant they belonged to the member of Court who'd given it to her, a symbol of ownership and property.

Ramses let it dangle. "This... well, this means something. To those people, I mean." He paused, throwing his head in the direction of the school. "It also makes whoever wears it invisible."

Because they'd be just another body around here, another girl fawning over the Court boys. I pushed hair behind my ear. "You want me to wear that?" He nodded, and I swallowed. "You want me to be your girlfriend?"

"Fake girlfriend actually," he said, his cheeks suddenly very red. Ramses was usually pretty confident with things, but apparently not today. Without warning, he returned the thing to the box. "I'm sorry. This was a stupid idea and so out of line to ask—"

But it wasn't, and I showed him that when I got his wrist, the box with the necklace between us. Grabbing him made him stop, and when he did, I sat back. I cleared my hair from my neck. "You gonna make me put it on myself?"

His eyes widened. "You wanna do that? I mean." More throat clearing. "You wanna be my girlfriend?"

"Fake girlfriend, yeah." I nodded. "I think it's a great idea." Actually, it was beyond brilliant. He was right, this necklace would make me invisible. I'd be just another dopey girl to these people, and him taking me into Windsor House under this guise wouldn't raise any questions at all. I'd be his, and I guess he'd be mine.

Ramses swallowed. "You're sure? This would require a lot of acting."

Probably not as much as he thought, and I waited, nodding toward the necklace in the box. He didn't wait this time, taking it out, and when he came forward, I looked away, so this all wouldn't be so awkward for him.

Ramses Mallick surprisingly smelled really nice, familiar like the comforts of home. He felt safe, and that's something I didn't get a lot. I liked him there in that space. I liked his safety, truly.

He panned, facing me. "So we should probably have some terms, like is hand-holding okay?"

Definitely, and I showed him that when I took his hand. He laughed, that deep chuckle he did.

"Kissing?" he asked, bouncing those thick, brown eyebrows. He immediately shook his head with it, and I knew he was joking, but maybe I wasn't.

I swear to God, he looked like a deer in headlights when I not only rose up in my seat but grabbed his lapels.

"No sex," I said, then pressed my mouth against his. I started the kiss as a joke, my lips smiling against his, but eventually the expression fell. His mouth was too warm, that feeling of familiarity, that home. It reminded me of someone else, but the opposite. It wasn't scary or threatening. It didn't *scare me*, the feelings that came behind it.

It was over when Ramses bunched fingers in my hair, his hand the same on my back. He had easily a full fist of my coat, and I had somehow made it onto his lap. I had no idea if he'd pulled me or if I'd slid over myself.

Long fingers looped around my dark strands. "No sex," he promised, then returned me to my side of the car. He turned the car off after that, and when he came around to my side and let me out, I knew today's show was about to begin.

CHAPTER
TWELVE

Royal

"What the fuck is this?" Jax directed our group in another direction, and my arm left Mira's shoulders for the same reason. What the fuck *was* this?

Hell no.

Voices… my name being called as I stalked away from my friends. I made out Jax's voice among them, telling me to stop, as well as LJ's and Knight's. They were shouting behind me, Mira too, which I didn't give a shit about as I walked away. The only thing that concerned me right now currently came down the hallway, their hands together like they were a fucking thing.

They weren't a fucking thing.

But that necklace around her neck told different, that shine around her neck that immediately elicited a stab in my insides. I saw no reasoning in these moments, heard no words from my friends calling me to come back. I just stalked across that hallway.

And I threw that fucker Mallick against the lockers.

"Royal!" December's voice this time, her hand ripping me away from this piece of trash. Ramses Mallick may have height, but I had the size factor. I could crush his lanky-ass body like a toothpick.

"Prinze, what the fuck?" he seethed, pushing me off him. "What the hell's your problem?"

"You know what the hell's my problem." I cut in front of December, the girl *literally* freaking out on me. She screamed in my ear, tugged at my jacket, but I didn't care. I held her back. "You stay away from her."

"Stay away?" Ramses looked me up and down. "Go ease off your fucking 'roids, dude. She's my girlfriend."

His... girlfriend.

No fucking way.

Ramses pushed me again, and this time, I let him, the shock rattling me or something. Clear of me, Ramses reached for December, and not only did she take his hand, but went under his arm when he pushed it around her.

Pain, extreme pain pulsed through me, and even more so when Mallick tightened his hold on her.

He rubbed her arm, jutting a chin in my direction. "What happened to your eye, bro?"

My eye...

I faced away only to come back to a smirk, Mallick.

He secured his hold around December tighter. "You run into a wall or something?"

Screams... December's voice again, but this time, they were warranted. I knocked Mallick to the ground with a single punch, to *his* eye.

I guess we hit the same damn wall.

CHAPTER
THIRTEEN

December

The hallway flooded in chaos, guys and girls everywhere. Windsor Prep girls were screaming while Windsor Prep guys, on the other hand, were cheering things on. Meanwhile, Ramses, Royal, and I were in the middle of it. *I* was trying to pull Royal off Ramses only for Ramses himself to get the upper hand, and then I had to pull *him* off Royal. Eventually, I had to give up on them both, *literally* screaming at them both to stop, and I got no help from anyone. Especially Knight, LJ, and Jax. A force, the three boys held the crowds off while the boys in front of me attempted to kick the shit out of each other. Clothes were torn, Royal at one point with his jacket completely off and his buttons pulled to the state where his chest exposed. Ramses managed to keep his clothes on, but as kempt as he looked this morning, the damage was done between the scuffle on the floor and the blood from his lip. Royal had gotten him not just in his eye, but his mouth as well and looked like he was about to go for the other eye until Mr. Pool, our English teacher, came into the hallway. The students there for the fight divided immediately, and Jax, Knight, and LJ who'd been aiding the fight by keeping the crowds back released their impenetrable hold on the other students. They stood back, allowing Mr. Pool to come in, and as soon as he did, he grabbed both Ramses and Royal by their clothing.

"Get up." He scowled, returning both guys to their feet. After he got them grounded, he forced distance between them both. "What do you two think you're doing?"

They said nothing, snorting like bulls at each other. Mr. Pool pushed them forward. "To the headmaster's office. Both of you, and to the rest of you, back to class before you join them."

That cleared out the hallway real quick, all but me, LJ, Knight, and Jax. Horror-struck, even Mira left with friends, the girl whimpering in her hands, but the three boys and I stayed. I didn't think we knew what to do after that.

I had no idea what just happened.

———

I got Mr. Pool to give me a hall pass during second period English. I was taking his English Lit-8 class this semester and wanted to know the fallout regarding the boys, so color me surprised when Principal Hastings's office was still occupied nearly over an hour after the scuffle in the hall. I figured they'd all be done in there by now, and not only were they not done, multiple voices beyond Royal's and Ramses' could be heard outside. I knew because I poked my head in on the secretary to ask if I could ask Principal Hastings a question. I made up some excuse for the reason why, and while standing there, other voices could definitely be made out. One of which I distinctly remembered as being Royal's dad.

Christ.

This thing was getting out of control, and Ramses and I

were only fake girlfriend/boyfriend for less than two hours. After my initial poke and not so subtle spying, I stayed in the hallway outside of the headmaster's office. Waiting was the only way I'd know for sure what happened.

I didn't have to wait long.

The door blew open just long enough for me to clear, and I stayed behind it, Royal and his dad coming out into the hall behind the door's glass window. A coat over his arm, Mr. Prinze threw it on.

He pointed a finger at Royal. "We're going to deal with this at home. Get out to the car."

Royal had his hands in his pockets, and though I couldn't see his response, he did have his blond head slightly down. He shrugged. "I have to get my stuff first."

His father threw his hands up and I braced myself, and I noticed Royal stiffen too. It wouldn't be the first time his dad had struck him. I'd witnessed an occurrence firsthand, but it seemed in this case, Mr. Prinze only raised his hands out of frustration.

"Straight to the car after," he said, then stalked the opposite way down the hallway. With him clear, I closed the door, and I think it'd been the noise that forced Royal to turn my way. He stared right at me, stiffening again.

I stared too.

It'd been for a different reason, I'd wager, his eye taking my attention. True, Ramses had gotten his licks in on Royal. He had a bruise the size of a state on his cheek, and his clothes he'd returned to their proper places on his body, but they were still ripped and torn. Ramses had definitely gotten him good, but he hadn't done that, his eye. That'd been there before the fight.

That may have even started the fight.

Catching me looking at his black eye, Royal avoided eye contact and, returning his hands to his pockets, stalked around me with just as much force as his dad had on the opposite side of the hallway. He was running away, *avoiding me*, but he wasn't going to get away that easy.

I stalked after him too. "Royal Prinze, you have some nerve."

The hall silent besides us, he continued to move, but I didn't let him. I grabbed him by the arm, turning him and making him face me. "What's your problem?" I shot, seething. "You think you have some kind of ownership on me? Like you have any right at all to do such a thing because of me?"

He turned but I cut in front this time. If he was going to avoid this conversation, he'd have to go through me this time. I put hands on my hips. "What *the hell* is your deal? Because if this is some kind of savior complex because Paige was your friend and I'm her sister, I call bullshit on that. You don't care about me. You've shown that on more than one occurrence, and not only did you hurt Ramses *again* today, I think you did it as just another power play. To throw your weight around like you did with that fucking haze—"

"You know nothing." He moved, but I pushed him back this time. His eyes narrowed. "Back off, December."

"You back off." I pushed him again for good measure, and though he stayed his ground, he looked about two seconds from exploding. Good. I got up in his face. "You're a jerk and you're cruel and you're so out of line regarding this thing with Ramses it's not even funny. He didn't do anything wrong. He's with me, and if you think you have any right to do anything about that, you have another thing fucking coming. Newsflash, Royal Prinze, you don't own me—"

"Well, maybe you own me!"

I blanched, completely thrown off by what he said. It took me a moment to realize he'd even said it...

But he had, and I knew just as well as he stood in front of me. He was shaking, seething himself. He threw fingers into his hair. "Never mind."

No never mind, and I got hands on him again, making him face me.

He swallowed. "You don't know anything, and you're definitely understating the potential of that guy who fucking goaded me first. Ramses Mallick was a *jerk* when he went to school here, December, and I know that just as well as many of the guys here. They haven't forgotten. None of us have, and do you know what they wanted to do to him because of that? What they would have done if not for me in order to get that ring on his finger?"

I didn't, shaking my head. "What?"

He leaned in. "They wanted to *beat him*, whip him with an actual whip until his skin fell off, and even then, I don't know if it would have stopped."

My stomach turned, sickness brewing, and Royal only worked his jaw.

"He was a bully," he said, stepping back. "Facts, and no amount of turning over a new leaf would make people around here forget that. Memories run deep here, so don't for a fucking second let that guy you're apparently dating off as being some goddamn saint in this place—"

"So why did you stop it, then?" I asked, in his face again. I was so close. "Why did you intervene? Why not hurt him like the rest? Why… why did you say what you just said to me?"

That I owned him… That I could possibly in this place and with who he was? This powerful boy could never be owned. He was cruel…

Right?

The lines were starting to blur here, and nothing made sense, especially Royal when he grabbed my arms, forcing me to look up at him.

"I think you know why, Em," he said, and steps coming down the hall, he let go of me. He stared over my shoulder, and when I turned, his dad stood there. I had no idea how much he'd seen, but his expression wasn't at all happy.

"Is there a problem?" the man asked, and Royal immediately put distance between us.

Royal put hands behind his back. "No problem, sir. I'm getting my things."

So formal, so submissive. The state of Royal's eye took my sight again, a dark mark Ramses didn't inflict. He'd gotten it from someone else.

Mr. Prinze faced me now. "Good. You've got one minute and one only."

Royal nodded, his dad finally leaving. Royal started to go too, but I called him. I had more questions, so many more, and I didn't want him to go. He stopped again, but this time, it looked like it hurt him to do it.

"I have to go," he said, averting his eyes from me. "I'm suspended."

He left me with only that before escaping down the hallway and around a corner, and I would have gone after him again if not for further commotion in the hallway. The headmaster's office had opened again, and this time Ramses and another man came out.

"Unbelievable," said the man donned completely in a gray suit. A wool jacket over his arm, he pushed arms through it. "You just got here, and you're already getting into crap."

I hadn't seen the mayor of Maywood Heights this close up before, but I definitely recognized him from Ramses' holiday party. Ramses was a mash-up of ethnicities, his golden complexion so obviously from his father. The man was older, salt-and-pepper hair perfectly pushed back and polished. I wondered if he had curls too, but if he did, he made sure they were in order. He wasn't happy at all like Royal's dad, and Ramses appeared just as unsettled.

"Sorry, Dad—"

"You're sorry," said Mayor Mallick, huffing when he got his coat together. "Ramses, just when I feel like you're finally starting to get things together..." He stated this with a sigh, shaking his head. "You just keep disappointing, boy."

Ramses always sounded so whatever about his father, annoyed, and I had caught him a time or two in anger. I hadn't blamed him considering the history father and son had, but when Mayor Mallick said what he had, the words did play on Ramses' expression in a different away. He looked almost guilty when he pushed hands into his pockets.

"I'm sorry," he repeated, and Mayor Mallick shook his head again.

He looked at Ramses. "Your uncle can't bail you out of things every time—"

Out of the office came Principal Hastings this time, and the man in the spectacles waved a hand.

"One more thing, Ibrahim," he said to the mayor, so informal. Together, the two men went back into the office, and after closing the door, Ramses threw out a breath. He turned on his heels, and when he found me, he bunched a hand into his curls. They no longer held that precision, and though his lip had stopped bleeding, his own dark eye was starting to surface.

He frowned. "How much of that did you see?"

Enough, I came forward. "Your dad in there?"

Ramses nodded, facing the door. "Just when I think I'm starting to get on his good side," he said with a laugh, a joke but the smile didn't quite reach his eyes. He pushed a hand behind his neck. "I'm in deep, 'Zona. Not gonna lie."

"You're suspended?" I asked, knowing Royal's sentence.

Ramses bobbed his head twice. "Not as long as Prinze, but we both are out of here for a little bit. I only think I got off a little light because I didn't start it—"

"And apparently because of your uncle?" I asked, and his eyes widened.

"Heard that too, huh?"

"Yeah. Who is it? Your uncle?"

In the next seconds, the door opened again, and two men returned, Principal Hastings and Mayor Mallick. Both men had been talking, but as soon as they saw Ramses and me, they stopped immediately. Their sights drifted over to my direction, and after a silent exchange, the mayor put a hand over Ramses' shoulder.

"We should probably go, son," he said, then gave Principal Hastings a nod.

The headmaster did the same, and Ramses was basically dragged away.

"I'll text you," he said to me, lifting a hand, and it wasn't long before the headmaster was waltzing up right on me.

His eyes narrowed. "Do you have a pass for lingering in the hallway, Ms. Lindquist?"

I actually did, and after showing it to him, he returned back into his office. I got a text on the way back to class, and once I did, I almost dropped my phone.

My uncle is our stuffy old headmaster, Ramses' text said. *I thought you knew?*

CHAPTER
FOURTEEN

December

Birdie: So were you going to mention that you and Ramses were dating or…

    Me: It's new. Just kind of happened.

    Birdie: Just kind of happened, huh? *winky smile*

    Me: Oh, shut up.

    Birdie: But for serious, tho. How you going to leave your girls out of this? Kiki and Shakira are livid.

    Me: I told you. It just kind of happened and wasn't malicious. Honestly, now I'm kind of wishing we kept things on the DL after today.

    Birdie: Right? I mean, what was up with Royal? WTF.

    Me: Yeah…

    Birdie: You guys just had a casual hookup, right? That one time? Weird of him to be all jelly.

    Me: Yeah.

    Birdie: I swear to God everyone is losing their minds around here. First Ramses wants to join Court and then you guys? Any more secrets you wanna share? LOL

Me: Not particularly. I think I've had enough for a lifetime.

———

Text messages throughout the day with Birdie turned out to only be the start of the day that wouldn't seem to end. I'd heard from not just her but Shakira, Kiki, and a few of our other friends as well. They all had the same questions, the same intrigue about something even I was confused out. Matters only became worse at lunchtime when I somehow had become the center of a gossip invasion not just from our friends but any and everyone who seemed to suddenly want to sit at our table. People used excuses, of course, but it was hard not to notice people listening in on conversations with Birdie, the rest of our friends, and me. When I figured out those sudden ulterior motives, I kept silent, letting my friends talk while I ate. I evaded people most of the day and basically hid entirely in gym class. I'd gone out of my way to avoid Mira and her friends on any day, but today, the day her boyfriend decided to hit my new boyfriend...

And say all kinds of things to me.

It was all completely fucked up what Royal said in the hall this morning, and I wanted to block it all out instantly the minute I'd heard it. I found I couldn't no matter how many conversations I tried to blend in to or how many classes I tried to pay attention in. Royal said what he said.

Well, maybe you own me...

Later that evening, I played with Hershey when I got yet another text message after the day from hell, and seeing it was Ramses, my eyes widened. I figured his phone access might be limited after his suspension.

Ramses: Hey, I'm outside. Come out.

Come out.

A flash of the curtains told me he was outside, his Benz

running in the driveway, and I placed Hershey on the floor, then got my coat on. I took her with me downstairs, and after telling Rosanna I was going outside for a bit, I bore the chill out to the warm Mercedes. When I got inside, Ramses had his seat warmers on, which felt pretty frickin' good with the car's heating.

I clicked the door shut, and Ramses looked hella worse for wear. He'd definitely seen better days, that bruise around his eye was purple, and noticing I stared at it, he gestured to it with a dismissive shrug.

"Looks worse than it feels," he said, passing it all off. He put his seat belt on. "You ready?"

"For what?"

He eyed me. "I, uh, told you I was taking you to Windsor House. After school? You forget already?"

That was still on? Honestly, I kind of thought those plans were dead after today.

Well, maybe you own me…

My heart raced at hearing the words, deep and hypnotic in my head, and I found myself staring outside. So much had changed in only a few hours, things that felt right before feeling weird now. I didn't know how exactly things changed. I just knew they did.

Things did feel weird now, things I was going to do or say definitely weird. Things like going to Windsor House…

Things like this necklace around my neck.

I played with it, very aware of Ramses patiently waiting beside me. He stared at me, his figure in my periphery.

"Do you not want to do this today?" he asked, and when I faced him, he frowned. "If we don't right now, I don't know when I can. My dad freaked the fuck out. Like seriously lost his shit. The only reason I'm out now is because he and my mom are out to dinner with some of my dad's staff. We might not get another chance for a while if we don't do this today."

I moved in the seat. "You still think we should do this? That it's a good time?"

He passed a look like he didn't understand. "Why wouldn't it be? Like I said, we might not get another chance. I don't know what it is, but my dad went hard on me after we left the school. I mean, I knew he and my uncle would be like whatever—"

"Yeah, and what's up with that? Principal Hastings being your uncle?" Too weird. "You so didn't mention that."

"Never came up, I guess? He's my mom's brother, and honestly, outside of school, I don't really have a relationship with him. None of us do. He keeps to himself mostly."

I wouldn't want to be in casual conversations with the guy, not the best people person. I figured that was just because he was headmaster and that's how he was at school.

"Fuck, they handed me my ass." He put his head back. "That's why I got out after Royal and his dad. They were going over 'how I was better than that,' and I kind of just wrote it off. It wasn't until after I got to the car and my dad literally took everything he could away from me for the next two weeks I started to listen. I swear it's like a goddamn switch went off. In my uncle's office, I got limited car and social privileges. But the minute my dad and I were alone, he took away everything. I literally had to bribe our staff to give me the keys to my car and my cell phone tonight. I don't know what my dad's deal is. He's never been that strict, let alone cared."

Maybe things were different now that he was Court. Maybe he was held to a high standard like many of the dads did here apparently. Royal's dad was terrible.

You own me...

I clicked my seat belt on, and turning in his seat, Ramses sat up.

"Changed your mind?" he asked, and I just told him to

drive. I did have a reason for wanting to go to Windsor House. That was the only thing that hadn't changed.

The drive over was pretty silent between Ramses and me, Ramses doing most of the talking. He wanted to go over objectives, like what we both should be acting and doing once we were there. We both took the position that we should try to blend in, and if there were opportunities to ask anything, we should do so with caution. He planned to corner a few of the guys and get some good questions in. I, on the other hand, wanted to talk to Royal myself. There were some things so off going on here, off about him and the things he was both saying and doing. His actions were definitely doing one thing, but his words were saying something entirely else. I wanted to talk to him, get a read on him.

I wanted to know the truth.

Now, whether that truth would come out tonight, I didn't know, but I wanted to try as Ramses let us into the steel gates of Windsor House. People weren't playing out on the lawn today despite there being no snow. I guess too cold, a hard chill before the temperatures warmed and the flowers came out for spring. I hoped that day would start to come soon, too many of these cold, cold days. We pulled up the cobblestone walk, and after getting out, Ramses came around the car. He guided us from the garages up to the front door and seemed to navigate the winding property pretty well considering he'd never been Court before. I asked him about that, and he shrugged.

"Any guy worth his weight in this town has been coming here since we were kids. They, the fathers and grandfathers, in this town try to get us knowledgeable about the brotherhood early."

This all sounded so cult-like it wasn't even funny, a thick bond, which I knew about, and Ramses put out a hand.

"You ready?" he asked, but his hand ended up lowering when I left him hanging.

"I need you to be completely transparent about some-thing," I said, thinking about something else. "What exactly did you do to some of the guys in there?"

"Do?"

I nodded. "You know the whole bully thing?"

There were a lot of things I let go after he told me he'd been one, but if what Royal said about him was true, then there was a reason they'd all planned such a cruel haze. It was a reason I definitely wanted to know, and though it wasn't my job to judge, those facts were needed on my end. They'd help me process a few things, one or two.

A sigh and Ramses was pushing a hand to his neck. "You wanna do this now?"

I knew what he said about the time he had out tonight, but I did. I leaned back against the door.

Another sigh before he tucked hands under his arms. "Mostly jostling."

"What kind?"

"Rumors. Calling guys shit behind their backs. Idle gossip."

"Okay."

"Then there were some other things." He lounged against the door too. "Things like screwing around with a guy's girl behind his back." He raised a hand. "Really, 'Zona, I'm not proud of it, and I don't do shit like that anymore. It's fucked up, and I know that. Happened to me at my last school, and I really know that."

He hadn't mentioned that about the last relationship he'd been in, but he'd been adamant about not wanting one while he was here. I guess there'd been a reason.

"I'm sorry that happened to you," I admitted.

He shrugged. "It is what it is, and I deserved it. I deserved a lot of things."

But had he deserved a beating? I chewed my lip. "What

did you do to Royal? *Did* you do something? Something specific beyond handling him?"

"You could say that." He pushed off the door, shaking his head. "I may have suspended him from a building."

What the fuck?

"What?" I asked. "Why?"

"Because I did and could. We were both fighting for number one around here. Anyway, he got his just desserts in the end."

"How?"

He took out his key. "He finished his haze, *that*, and I didn't."

All this was madness what these boys put each other through, and when Ramses put his key into the door, he waited before turning the knob. He put out his hand, and I stared at it again.

I pushed my hands into my coat. "Let's just keep things casual in here, okay? I don't want to create any more waves."

I didn't want any more fights, and though I think he understood that, his expression did shift. He passed it off quickly, though, donning his signature Ramses grin before lifting a hand over me to move forward. He turned the knob, and not only did those wide doors open, so did the grandness of the place inside. I'd never officially come through this way, crystal chandeliers above glistening the hallways. Immediately, a staff member aided us by taking our coats, and after we denied drinks, Ramses guided us through the official headquarters of the Court. I'd been told the Court used it for all their business dealings and events, but it was also where the younger members hung out. I'd lived here for a short time, but never came down to really mingle.

For obvious reasons.

I'd been basically kidnapped the first two times, and the last, not any better. The place was pretty frickin' beautiful, though, classic with its wood panel walls and hardwood floors. The place shined like polished oak, and immediately, Ramses' and my presence was known and traveled through hallways filled with both boys and girls. The girls wore neck-laces, some in packs without their guys, and I hoped to God we wouldn't be seeing Mira today. If so, I believed another epic throwdown would be going, but this time between Court-kept girls. I had no beef with her at the present, but I found it hard to believe she wouldn't have a few questions and/or take a few shots at me after what happened with Royal and Ramses. I wouldn't just let someone push me around, so I knew if she threw a shot, I'd be throwing one right back.

"Just be casual," Ramses said to me, greeting a few boys who came up to us, still wearing their academy uniforms. Ramses and I had changed out of ours, but I noticed quite a few people still had them on, even girls. I recalled Royal and Knight mentioning they lived here, and they might not be the only ones.

"So Mallick finally makes his appearance amongst the brotherhood," came a guy, a redhead who immediately grabbed and shook Ramses' hand. He had a couple others behind him, more boys who exchanged greetings with Ramses.

"I guess so." Ramses grinned at the acknowledgment, snapping when he came out of it. He clearly knew these guys, whether from school or whatever I didn't know, but not only was he friendly with them, they did the same, which got me thinking about something Royal said again. He told me these guys wanted to beat him up for his past.

Well, it seemed all that was under the bridge now, the phoniness of this place quite frankly pissing me off. More than one guy waved over to Ramses, and after Ramses intro-duced me as his girlfriend, they were suddenly wanting to pull him into more conversations.

"We got to talk about what happened today, dude," said

the redhead. He looked around. "You and Royal getting into it? You're bold, dude."

Ramses bunched his curls. "Yeah, it was pretty dumb. Got us both suspended and me put under lock and key."

"I'll bet." Redhead smacked his chest. "What was it really about? We heard, uh…"

The guy took notice of me, and immediately, Ramses raised a hand.

"Really, just an old beef. We should be past it now." Ramses' lips pressed tight, and noticing that, the redhead and his friends smiled. They immediately moved away when all of the sudden familiar faces came into the room.

LJ and Knight dominated, two girls under each of their arms. They got bro hugs of acknowledgment right upon crossing into the space, and suddenly the redhead and his friends weren't so bold themselves. They stepped back from Ramses, averting their eyes from LJ and Knight. I had no idea where Jax or even Royal was, but tonight, the presence of those two seemed to be enough to make the redhead step back.

Ramses didn't make a move, and neither did I as suddenly LJ and Knight were very aware of us. They dropped arms from their girls, coming over, and when LJ raised a hand, I braced myself. I figured I'd have to step in yet again, but not only did LJ and Knight stop a safe distance away from Ramses, LJ kept his hand raised. He held it for a shake.

Ramses gave it to him.

They both brought it in, hugging too despite the stiff look from Ramses. He instantly locked up but did give into it. After the shake with LJ, Knight gave him the same. They fist-pounded after.

"Good you made your way over," said LJ, deliberately not looking at me. Knight did the same too, standing beside his friend. He always played the position of bodyguard in their group. Something I definitely noticed. LJ waved a hand. "You been to the clubhouse yet?"

"Actually." Ramses moved a hand behind me, but he didn't touch me. He was keeping things cool like we discussed outside. He smiled. "I got December with me, so…"

The clubhouse must have been the boys-only section that I'd actually been inside. The guys themselves had let me in.

This didn't seem to be the case now, LJ's head rising and dropping. "Another time, then…"

"Actually, why don't you go?" I suggested, needing the space. I forced my own smile. "Need to go to the bathroom anyway."

Ramses passed a polite look to the others before facing me. "It can wait."

"It shouldn't," I emphasized. He'd probably be able to speak more candid with me not around anyway.

Understanding that, he nodded. He allowed the guys to take him away, the whole group going, and I used that invisibility being a Court kept as promised. I walked right out of that room and barely anyone took notice of me.

I got all the way to Royal's door with barely even a glance.

I tapped, nothing forceful like before. I had different objectives now.

Things were so different.

They were in so many ways and my heart in my throat, I waited for Royal to answer the door. After a few moments of me standing there, I tried again, sighing. "Royal? Royal… it's me."

Absolutely nothing, literal ringing in my ears. He either was ignoring me or wasn't there.

"You lost or something?"

Down the hall came yet another familiar face, one filled usually with jokes and humor, but not today. Jax had a girl under his arm too, the pair of them basically all over each other. He had her close while she felt up his abs, but seeing me, he let go of her.

I folded my arms. "No. Just seeing what's up with Royal. Is he in?"

He smirked at me, actually smirked before shaking his head. "No, he's not."

He started to walk away, but I followed.

"Any idea when he'll be back?" I asked, raising and dropping my hands. I got it. He wasn't happy. Royal was his friend, and he was taking his position after the fight. Hell, he'd even egged it on, holding people back while the guys went at it like animals.

Where LJ and Knight hadn't acknowledged me at all, Jax chose chill, giving it completely to me. He frowned. "Sorry, I don't. Moved out. He ain't here no more."

He did walk away this time, leaving me standing there. Royal moved out.

So what did I do now?

CHAPTER
FIFTEEN

December

The night at Windsor House turned out to not be fruitful at all. Maybe if we'd had more time, had done things differently.

Maybe if I had.

Ramses got a tour. That was it, and after, his frustration lay with lack of information whereas mine stemmed from something else entirely. The thing was, I couldn't even voice those frustrations. I couldn't tell him the truth, what Royal had said to me outside that hallway, and where I felt things should go from here. I had let him think everything was fine, and since he was suspended, that only made the guise easier. I was lying to more than one person now.

I was on my own now.

I actually tried not to be, going out of my way to run into the people who surrounded Royal on his day-to-day. Knight, LJ, and Jax's presence continued to be prevalent around the halls of Windsor Prep, but like at Windsor House, they wanted nothing to do with me. Any direct approaches resulted in them walking the other way, and any indirect, an accidental bump in the hall or surprise around the corner, they passed off. They clearly didn't want to talk to me, but I didn't care.

I got an opportunity during fourth period.

Study hall happened every day for me during that time, but that day, I decided to take it in the library instead of bull-shitting outside with friends. Study hall usually tended to be the period Shakira, Birdie, and I blew off to sneak a smoke or two behind the bleachers. I found I needed the ease of a high more and more the last few weeks, but instead of smoking weed that day, I decided to study. I didn't have Dr. Brain, aka Ramses Mallick, anymore to coach me study tips at lunch. I had to study now to get myself through this final semester, and I guess someone else chose to do that too.

Jax came in around halfway through the period, not surprising, but when he did, he did so alone. He had none of his clique with him, completely by himself, which was a rare occurrence in itself. These boys always had people around them but not today. He pulled out what looked to be a stack of comic books from his bag, popping in a couple of AirPods while he read them, and escaping my table, I grabbed my bag and came over. I'd been alone today too, so that was easy. I sat right down next to him.

He barely looked at me.

The ass literally passed me a single glance before dampening his finger and turning the page of his comic book. I was over it, over him completely, but as I needed him at the present, I got a notebook out. I wrote a note, sliding the whole notebook over.

Got a few questions, the note said, and though I noticed his gaze slide over to it, the connection didn't stay. Sighing, I wrote another note. I pushed it over.

Me: I want to talk to him.

Dismissive, Jax ignored me again. I nudged him with the notebook, and all it did was cause his jaw to clench.

Me: Please.

He stared at that one, stared at it long and hard before finally taking his AirPod out and taking my pen.

Jax: Haven't you done enough?

Ouch, but I wasn't giving up since he was talking.

Me: Tell me where he is. It's important.

Jax: Sure.

Me: I'm serious, Jax.

Jax: I'm sure you are.

Me: Jax.

Jax: No.

Me: Please.

Jax: No.

Me: It's about Paige.

That got his attention. That got his everything, and suddenly, he wanted nothing to do with that pen. He turned away from me, comic back in his hand.

Me: I need to talk to him about Paige. I need to talk to him about a lot of things—

My pen lined across the page as suddenly Jax was grabbing his stuff, then me when he got me by the arm and took me behind a bookshelf. He let go when we were clear, but he wasn't giving me any distance.

He raised a finger. "You need to back off."

"Back off from what?" I asked. "What about Paige do you want me to back off from?"

What about Paige did he not want me to know? I obviously had my suspicions, but this was the first time I came forward with them. This was the first time I addressed them in any type of capacity outside of with Ramses.

Rising up, Jax scanned the area before eyeing me again. "If you think this is all a game or something you can just play around with, it's not, December."

"What's a game?" I asked, and when he looked away from

me, I got in his face. "Why would my sister's life be a game? Why would anything I know be a game—"

"You don't know anything, and I can't have this conversation with you."

He left me, but I followed after him. I left my things and everything, going right out into the hallway with him. "I need to talk to him, Jax. Please."

"No, December," he said, turning on his heels. "What you need to do is stay out of this. It's dangerous."

"What's dangerous?"

"Everything, and if you get involved and something happens to you too…"

He closed his lips, the halls completely silent between us. That ringing in my ears had returned, and I approached Jax.

I swallowed. "If you don't tell me where he is, I will rip this goddamn town apart until I find him. I'll make noise. I'll scream until he talks to me and tells me what I want to know."

I deserved that. I deserved *everything*, and Jax folded a hand over his face.

He dropped it. "Wait for my text," he said, adjusting his bag on his arm. "Because when I come for you, I won't wait."

CHAPTER
SIXTEEN

December

Before I left the library, I told Jax where he could come and get me, but he waited until nearly midnight before actually texting me...

And that was only to tell me he was outside.

My dad was in, so I had to take the way out of my room Royal himself had showed me. Paige and he used to sneak in and out of the house through my bedroom window before I came to stay here. Irony hit, I used this passage now, and by the grace of God, Hershey stayed quiet. I put her in her kennel so she could sleep while I was away.

"We're going to make this quick," Jax stated pretty much immediately after I got inside his car. I had to go down the street to get in since I didn't want him to park in the driveway for my dad to see. He started the car. "He doesn't know we're coming."

He didn't know? Maybe because Jax knew better. I highly doubted Royal wanted to see me.

Well, he was going to anyway.

I had so many questions it maddened. Especially after that confrontation with Jax. He drove swiftly, a red number with a loud exhaust. I had no idea the make and model. He'd stripped all that from the car, a custom job, but it looked really expensive just like everyone else's rides who attended Windsor Prep. He had money like everyone else, and I only didn't fight him on his speed since he was doing what I asked.

"Where is he?" I asked along the way. I couldn't see Jax's face, a hood over his head like we were about to rob some place. He came over in a black hoodie, not even wearing a coat tonight.

"His house, Lindquist," he said, then faced me. "His dad's making him stay there."

After the suspension maybe, and I wasn't surprised. Ramses' family had him under lock and key after all.

Sitting back with that, I faced the window, watching the scenery change from nice to nicer. The foliage was more designed, the houses bigger and with larger yards. Eventually, we ended up outside of a gated community, one Jax key-coded his way into, then down a street that made my dad's huge-ass house look like a fucking shack.

The homes were basically mini versions of Windsor House, small castles, and if not that, Victorians. The largest castle dwelled on the corner, but Jax stopped just short of that, pulling into a driveway next door. He clicked a button, and the garage door opened, revealing not one but two more luxury cars. One was a Lexus and the other a Mercedes SUV.

We parked between them.

"Why do you have a garage door opener to Royal's garage?" I unbelted, but wouldn't be surprised considering they were bros.

Jax smirked. "Maybe because it's not his garage but mine. Well, my moms' since this is their house."

He said *moms*, as in plural. Caused me to stop a beat but

not long. I mean, why would it? Jax stared at me like maybe people had in the past, but seeing I wasn't now, he got out of the car and I did too. He waved me over after he locked the garage, and instead of going inside the house, we went behind it. We cut across a yard gorgeously landscaped with potted plants, a rock garden, and even a koi pond. It was all lovely, his moms obviously having done a great job. We didn't stay there long because soon Jax was pushing through tight hedges and into the yard next door. *This* yard managed to trump even his, the castle next door, and Jax had to guide me with finesse just to work around all the design work and landscaping. There were actual sculpted hedges to look like animals and other various designs. Noticing me looking at them, Jax stopped.

"Royal's dad keeps up with them," he said, frowning. "They were his mom's. All of this."

I turned in the maze in wonder, and if I didn't know it now, his words confirmed where I was. We were in Royal's backyard.

We were at Royal's castle.

He lived in one like a real prince, steeples and everything like out of a storybook. He had a real castle in the middle of a suburban neighbor.

I buried my hands in my coat pockets, and without any more detours, Jax tour-guided me right up to the back door. He put a key code in, something he knew, and after the security disarmed, he was able to open the door with his key. He stopped a moment, texting inside a dark room, then with the flick of the light, he revealed a celebrity kitchen.

Polished marble and sparkling countertops graced my eyes, a fruit display in the center of the kitchen island. I wasn't able to observe them long, Jax guiding me along the way. He spun a set of keys on his finger as he walked, and focusing on that, I nearly screamed when a cat the size of a mini tiger skated past my leg.

I had to cover my mouth and everything, a freaking jungle cat with a long tail and spots just casually walking down the hallway.

Jax looked at me over his shoulder, smirking when he noticed yet another holdup. He hunkered down to that big ole animal and ran his hand down its back. The thing appreciated it, purring before falling over. Jax scratched behind its ears. "Don't let Dinah intimidate you. She's a big softy."

She was big and I guess maybe soft like he said. She didn't even bite at him, clearly familiar with him as she leaned into his touch. He stood. "Let me go see what the holdup is. I texted him we're here. Don't know what's keeping him."

I figured that'd been who he texted in the kitchen, and nodding, I chose to stare at the walls while he went somewhere else in the house. I didn't wander far, fearing I'd get lost, and in any sense, the photos in the hall stole my attention anyway.

There were so many, lots of Royal through the years. There were some of him as a little kid, a small boy with sandy blond hair and always seemed to have some type of athletic gear in his hands. He played many sports over his various ages, football, lacrosse of course, and soccer. He even skied, and in that photo, he was with a few other people. One I immediately recognized as his dad. He looked the same, his hand on top of Royal's head. That's how young Royal was in the picture.

I stepped up, studying the other two people, a young girl not blond but red. She was on a set of skis with polls in her hands, grinning at the camera and slightly taller than Royal. Behind her was a woman, also redheaded and with the most gorgeous smile. She hugged both the girl and Royal, a pair of ski goggles on her face. The whole family stood in front of a snowy backdrop, the note *Vale, Colorado* stamped in the corner and with a year, a year a long time ago.

I ventured back, the wide expanse of hallway filled with pictures of the girl and the woman with the beautiful smile.

They always were together and with Royal, the three of them peas in a pod. Royal's dad was in some of the photos, but they were mostly just the three of them. The majority of them consisted of Royal and the young girl from the baby stage to around eight or nine. The girl was clearly older, Royal a year or two behind in every photo. I noticed eventually, though, Royal's photos started to age. He got older, by himself, and the photos of the girl and the woman stopped. It was like they were frozen in time while Royal continued on, by himself through the ages.

"Why are you here, December?"

Royal behind me and Jax *behind him* when I turned. The pair stood in the hallway, both brooding, but Royal could have taken the award. He wasn't happy, wearing a robe and with wet hair. I guess that'd been where he was when Jax texted.

Royal frowned. "Why is Jax saying you're asking about Paige?"

Maybe because I was and started to move when he stalked toward me. His robe silk, it parted off him with his heavy strides.

That's when I saw the bruises.

They chased completely up his right side, a large surface area across his ribs and abs. He even had a few punches to the chest, and I honestly hadn't believed the fight with Ramses had been that bad. It *wasn't* that bad. I'd been there. The robe settled the moment he crossed the hallway, but by the time that happened, I was taking inventory of his face. Ramses had gotten him on the cheek that day at school, but that was it.

Royal had two black eyes now, the left side even worse than the right, and the new cut on his lip wasn't bleeding but it was there. He honest to God looked like he'd been in a car accident.

He honestly looked like someone beat the shit out of him.

Someone obviously had, and for whatever reason, I

grabbed his robe. I needed to see the damage. I needed to *see* what someone had done to him.

"December," he warned, but I noticed he didn't stop me. He let me look, the garment falling off his muscled shoulder. He had a bruise there too.

"Your dad?" I questioned, knowing the truth when I covered it.

He shrugged. "Old man doesn't like fighting."

How ironic since he hit his son, and in the distance, Jax lounged against the wall. His eyes averted, but he was completed privy to this conversation.

"You didn't come here to ask me about my dad," Royal said, forcing me to look directly at him. He scanned me, my eyes, my mouth, and I wanted to push him. I wanted to shove him for affecting me and complicating my feelings. I wanted to yell at him, yell at him so bad, but when he looked like this? *Beat up* like this? Royal's nostrils flared. "You came to talk to me."

I did, but staring into two black eyes rattled my nerve. It *brought me* pain, and I hated it. I wanted to hate him, but he made it so goddamn hard. I blinked over cloudy eyes. "I did come to talk to you."

"So talk." He approached, a jump in his throat as he looked at me again. He stared all over my face, as if memorizing every flaw and every freckle. As if *seeing me* for me. "Say what you have to say."

I swallowed, finding I couldn't, and in those moments, he walked away, passing Jax. He was done with this conversation. He was done letting me try to talk, and I lost my window.

"I just need to know one thing."

He stopped, my voice causing him to turn back and peer over his shoulder. I didn't waste the opportunity this time, tears in my eyes as I approached him. I was glad my vision was cloudy and couldn't see him well. What I had to say scared the ever-living shit out of me, and I didn't know if I could face him full on.

"Is what happened that night," I started, swallowing and blinking down tears. "Is what happened that night with Paige at Route 80 something she chose? No one made her. No one had it out for her. It was something she chose to do?"

Because at the end of the day it was a choice, the reality of which ripped me apart. That my sister *chose* to be out there. That she made a choice…

Just like Ramses and Royal before him.

All of the boys before did. They *all* did what they wanted, and knowing my sister, she would have been the same. No one would have been able to stop her that night. Not if she truly wanted to do something.

It made me want to throw up just thinking about it, but I waited. I waited for Royal to speak and to tell me the goddamn truth.

"Tell me, goddammit." Full-on crying now, the tears streaming down my face. "Was my sister out there because she made a choice?"

It was obviously the wrong one, one that went bad, and he knew the truth. If he did, he needed to tell me, and finally, he turned around, that rough exterior completely gone. Emotion filled his eyes to the point he needed to squeeze them, a torture lining his face I'd never seen. It brought out the emotion in me, the sickness rising again.

His throat jumped. "I *begged* her not to, Em."

My breath caught, wavering right there in the hall. From behind, Jax's arms moved from in front of his chest. He didn't approach, lingering in the distance, but he was watching this.

He was there for a fallout.

He was there for Royal, Royal's hands coming up to grab mine. He squeezed them. "I begged her to the point of getting on my knees. I pleaded there was another way, another way to…"

"To what?" The ache I heard in my voice, more tears blinking down my face. Royal captured my cheek, wiping them away.

"To get revenge," he said, that emotion in his eyes making him blink. "She wanted revenge, December."

Revenge... something I wanted not long ago but now felt like a lifetime away. My mind was a haze, and I didn't know what to do with it all. I didn't know what to do about him or this or anything that happened.

I gripped his hand, but he wouldn't let me hold it long. He let go, putting distance between us. He shook his head. "I'll never forgive myself. I should have fought harder, fought her."

"Royal—"

He shook his head. "Please stay out of this, Em. Forget about what you think you know about it, and *stop* talking about all this. You need to get out of this town and as far away as you can get from me after graduation. I couldn't do this anymore if you got hurt too."

He hadn't explained with "this" was, but I had a feeling it was darker than I ever wanted to question. It was darker than I could even think, and before I knew it, Royal was talking to Jax down the hallway. They were whispering something, something about making sure I got home safe. Royal had said that part, and after he left Jax, Jax came to me.

His expression was grave, his hands in his hoodie pockets. "I'm going to take you home and after, this needs to end between you two. You're making things worse for him right now, worse for all of us."

I wanted to ask him in what way. I had so many questions, but hell if he let me ask them. He passed me, leaving me there in the hallway. Royal had been long gone, off somewhere in the house, and eventually, I had to leave too. There was nothing else to do.

They were clearly shutting me out of whatever this was.

CHAPTER
SEVENTEEN

December

I drove downtown in my sister's Ranger Rover, taking a second to breathe with my hands on the wheel. I was about to embark on something I might not be able to come back from. Something that scared the boys, something having to do with what happened to Paige. I knew I wouldn't be able to get anything out of them, so I was trying the next best thing...

Knocking on doors myself.

The only clues I had regarding my sister's intent to even be out at Route 80 at all that night came from Royal. He'd said she wanted "Court involvement." The "involvement" so obviously meant joining Court and she wanted to do so because he'd said she had gotten in a fight with someone, a girl she'd been seeing. He never told me who that girl was, but if my sister wanted to join the Court in order to do some kind of revenge on this girl, I wanted to know who she was. I wanted to stare her in the face and make her take some kind of responsibility. I idly wondered if I had already met this girl or at least, had seen her. She very well could have come over to California for my sister's services.

Here we go.

I slid my sister's journal off the passenger seat, gathering another shuddered breath. I wagered, out of all people, my sister's counselor, Lena Hastings, may know something about the people my sister used to hang with. I knew she hadn't worked with Paige since her freshman year, but that didn't mean the counselor didn't keep up with her. This was a moderately small town, and considering my sister's friends wouldn't talk to me, maybe her counselor would.

She gave me her journal after all.

Google said Principal Hastings's wife had a small practice she operated out of in the heart of Maywood Heights. It was actually right down the street from city hall and held a view of the hall's steeple and several shopping centers.

Lena Hastings, PhD, LCPC

Standing back from the door, I checked to see if I had to be buzzed up or anything, but since the door was unlocked, I went ahead and let myself inside. The walk up led to several businesses behind wooden doors, and I found Mrs. Hastings's office easily between an attorney's office and a massage therapist.

I poised my hand to knock only to have the door open in my face. A woman stood before me, a woman with long, dark hair and sparkling blue eyes and I nearly said something to her until a literal doppelganger came in beside her.

I swore to God I saw double, two of Lena Hastings staring at me. One wore yoga pants with stars and galaxies on them, her top nothing but a workout bra. She'd opened the door and had a coat in her hands, staring at me with wide eyes, while the other Mrs. Hastings wore something a little less casual. Her suit made her look like a working professional, her dark hair up, and widening the door, Professional Mrs. Hastings came around to see what the holdup was. Seeing me, she smiled, placing hands on her doppelganger's shoulders.

"December, hello," Mrs. Hastings said, the one in the suit, not the yoga gear. Her grin widened. "Why, how nice of you to visit."

I panned between the two women, mirror images of each other. After my initial shock of finding two when I'd meant to meet one, I obviously concluded these women were twins. Uncanny. I'd seen twins before but never so ridiculously gorgeous. The women looked like they should be walking down a runway together, and I remembered holding similar thoughts when meeting Mrs. Hastings originally. She was simply stunning then, and her sister was now.

Her sister, the other Mrs. Hastings in the yoga gear, glanced between Mrs. Hastings and me. "December?" she asked, looking back at me. "December... Lindquist?"

I blanched but professional-looking Mrs. Hasting chuckled. "Yes, Daisy, and doesn't she look so much like her sister?" The woman's laughter again resembled wind chimes. "You'll have to forgive my darling twin. Her memory seems to escape her that one of my favorite students had a sister. Well, this is her, Daisy. December?"

They both knew my sister? My gaze shifted between the two, but the yoga Mrs. Hastings, or I guess Daisy, didn't. She stared right at me, full on.

"Right," Daisy said, her smile small before completely lighting up her eyes. She nodded. "You do look so much like her."

Silence between us all before Daisy covered her mouth. She laughed a bit before facing her twin. "Sorry. It's just... I didn't expect her. Why didn't you tell me you'd be seeing her?"

"I didn't know." Mrs. Hastings said this with nothing more than her warm smile. "But it's such a delight, though."

"Yes." Daisy's attention shifted to me. "And sorry. We

both knew your sister. I used to volunteer at the school. Help Lena out. Lena was the…"

"Prep team coordinator, yes," Mrs. Hastings confirmed. She squeezed Daisy's arms. "And my sister graciously helped me out. Your sister was a part of the program freshman year."

I recalled that picture, being surprised that my tomboy sister would be a part of something so social. Mrs. Hastings had been in that picture, but no doppelganger, no Daisy.

Swallowing hard, Daisy pushed hair out of her face before hugging her sister. "I have to go I'm afraid. I shouldn't have been here as long as I was."

She didn't say why she was here but that wasn't any of my business. She probably just came to visit her sister or something.

Mrs. Hastings squeezed her in return, kissing her cheek before framing her face. "Anytime, my love."

Daisy smiled, the expression a bit stiff. I quickly got out of her way so she could pass me, and though she did, she stopped in the hallway.

She lifted a hand. "It was so nice to see you, meet you, December."

"And you," I said, hugging the journal to my chest. "Any friend really I could meet of my sister's."

Smile tight again, Daisy gave me a wave before pushing her arms through her coat. She placed it on as she headed down the hall, and Mrs. Hastings widened the door for me.

"Well, come in," she urged, and I did, angling around her into an office that let in so much light. She had windows literally in the formation of rays of sunshine, perfect to let just the light in and not the chill of the season. Her office was professional but homey, couches and armchairs in one section while her desk and a couple other chairs were on the opposite side of the room. She also had a dance floor, and I eyed it.

More of that wind chime laughter in my direction when she noticed my attention on it. She pushed hair behind her ear. "I do music and dance therapy too. I guess you could call me a jack-of-all-trades."

I guess so, and when she reached for my coat, I took it off and gave it to her.

"Can I get you a drink or anything?" she asked, hanging my coat on a vintage coat hook. She grinned. "I have water. Soda?"

I passed on both, but if I changed my mind, I'd ask. I took a seat on a chaise lounge, and she joined me by sitting on the chair across from it.

She crossed her legs. "Now, to what do I owe this surprising, yet delightful visit from you? Have you decided to take me up on sessions? Therapy? I have some spots open next week…"

"Oh, no," I started, but closed my lips.

Do better.

Immediately reverting, I waved my hand. "I mean, I'm more so here to just talk about my sister in general. Stories about her and her life here before I arrived. You know, for now?"

This was better, making things seem like a casual and friendly visit to discuss memories regarding my sister. Like my initial plan with Ramses, I did need things to appear normal. I didn't know what was bothering the boys about me poking. But something did bother them, so any questioning I did needed to stay on the DL for now. If anything, so as not to get back to them that I was prying.

Mrs. Hastings's smile returned, her nod light before placing hands on her knee. "I understand, but I have to say, anything that was exchanged between your sister and me during her sessions is strictly confidential."

"I know. I guess I just…" I pulled the journal forward, showing it to her. "I wanted to talk about her with you as her friend, I guess? The journal really helped."

Sitting back, Mrs. Hastings's eyes crinkled hard in the

corners. "I see. Well then, this requires something a little less formal, then, doesn't it? Come. Let's get away from the therapy couch and to more casual seating. We'll talk there."

As it turned out, I liked the switch across her office to lounge chairs. It felt less therapist and patient and more talking about someone we had a mutual relationship with.

I took the seat with ease, studying the collection of photos Mrs. Hastings had on the end table and coffee table. There were many of her and her sister, Daisy, the two on vacation with each other in places like Paris, London, Australia, and even Disney World. They'd definitely been adults with no kids in that last photo, Mickey Mouse ears on their heads and the two with their arms around each other. They were obviously incredibly close and the sole picture she did have with Principal Hastings was their wedding photo. *That* was weird. I turned away, watching as Mrs. Hastings sat down with a cup of coffee.

"Your sister is nice," I said, as Mrs. Hastings blew the steam off her coffee. Seeing me notice her photos, the light shined across her face again.

"She is and very fun as you can see." She nudged her coffee cup toward the table, pointing out a few of the photos there. "She got me to go to all those places. I seriously hate flying."

"Really?"

"Oh, loathe it." Chuckling, she stirred her coffee. "Definitely more of the adventurous type."

Sounded like me and my sister. Paige had always been the one to do all the running, free unlike me. I found myself easily bound by mental handicaps when they came, where she just said to hell with any problems she had. They always so easily rolled off her back.

Mrs. Hastings placed her cup on the table. "So the journal helped? I'm glad. I didn't know if it would or not."

I ran my hand over the cover. "Leave it to my sister to doodle when she should be writing her feelings."

"Oh, those were her feelings, December. So many. Your sister was very expressive but in her own way."

"Can you tell me about her? I mean, not the therapy stuff, of course, but just who she was now. You know we lived apart."

"I do." That made her sad, the expression reflecting its way across her eyes. "She was very excitable, but I wouldn't say not happy. She had a lot of good support here. She and Royal Prinze were inseparable. And of course Lance Johnson, Knight Reed, and Jaxen Ambrose. I only counseled her freshman year, but there wasn't a place she went where those four didn't go too, real friends until the…"

I looked up, knowing why she didn't finish.

Her smile saddened. "I'm sorry. What I meant was they were really good friends. You didn't have to worry about Paige. At least, when I knew her. She was very determined, always there fighting for herself and others. Many people admired her."

I admired her too, my hand on the moleskin. "I know you counseled her freshman year, but did you know anything else about her?"

"In what way?" Crossing her legs, she leaned in.

I shrugged. "I don't know. About the stuff she was into now? Was she still on the prep team?"

"Not that I know of, and to be honest, I think she did that mostly as a favor to me. Turnout was never great for the program, and she did me a favor by joining. Your sister was so popular. She got so many of the girls at school to come out for it."

I smiled. "Anyone she was close to on the team or…" That might be my in, my everything. My sister had a predominately male relationship range, and if she did prep team this one year, a team full of girls, that might be where she'd met *the* one.

Thinking about it, Mrs. Hasting picked up her coffee. "Honestly, I can't remember. She could have. Why do you ask?"

I sat back casually. "I just want to talk to everyone who knew her. It really does help, the grieving process."

Looking at me, Mrs. Hastings lowered her cup. "I wish I could be of more help. I knew your sister, but it'd been a long time. I didn't keep up with her over the years as much as I would have liked. I had so many students at that time, December. I'm so sorry."

It wasn't her fault, and I did understand. Coming here was a long shot, and I did know that too.

Mrs. Hastings nodded toward my hands, and when she did, I gave her the journal. "Honestly, this may give you more clues about her depth. Who she was at her core and the things she couldn't always say. Even to me. She told so much in these drawings." Handing it back to me, she sat back. "I wish you luck, and if you ever need anything, to talk for real, please call me. I'm happy to help. Anything to help."

CHAPTER
EIGHTEEN

December

So many days eased into calm around me following that initial visit to Mrs. Hastings's office. I should be happy about that. I should be happy things were starting to feel normal around me for once. Days at my dad's house were easy, the two of us passing ships, and things at school were even easier. Hubert would drop me off. I'd go to class, and the fight between Ramses and Royal quickly became a distant memory to the other drama and scholastic events going on at the school. My life was finally *normal*.

But I was anything but happy.

I looked for any indicator, something that told my sister had a relationship with anyone else besides Royal and his friends. I got no help from them, not even bothering to ask. I'd been warned about getting involved, so there's no way they'd be helping on this. The trail was quickly running cold without resources, and anything I gathered on my own wasn't much. I actually went to the library at one point, searching yearbooks of all things. My sister's sophomore year didn't hold much and her junior year even less outside of sports. My sister had been a jock, point blank. She didn't associate with anyone outside of that, at least on paper. There was no trail, no history.

And Ramses was coming back today.

He'd texted me a few times over the course of his suspension, nothing major or anything. He wanted to know how things were going at school and if things had settled. He wanted to know the fallout and if *I* was okay. I hadn't told him about the confrontation with Royal the day of the fight or even that I'd been over to see Royal. I didn't tell him anything. Mostly because I didn't know how to deal with him and what we initially had tried to do. I was so far away from our original plans now and, quite frankly, didn't know how to talk to him about that. My responses to him were very short over the two weeks of his suspension, the halls a buzz the closer he got to returning to school. Royal wouldn't be long behind, and though I didn't know his exact date, I assumed not far behind Ramses. He'd gotten a longer suspension since he started the fight, but no one knew for sure when he'd be coming back.

Actually, I was kind of nervous on the day of Ramses' return. I still was for all intents and purposes his "girlfriend," but so much had changed since we put that plan into action. Royal had basically admitted to me he wanted nothing to do with that haze, that he had tried to stop her but she did what she wanted to do. It'd been *Paige* who sought revenge on someone and over something she hadn't even shared with me, and exposing the Court…

Well, a lot of things had changed.

I waited in the hallway with friends, our meeting place before classes started. The whole school was whispering about Ramses coming back, and our friends were too, asking me how he'd been. I honestly couldn't tell them. I hadn't really talked to him, and overwhelmed by all the questions, I ended up making some sorry excuse before he even arrived. I said I had to get to class early or something, walking away, and I didn't even stay long enough to see what they thought about that. I didn't stay long enough to see Ramses. I was so lost and confused and just needed to get away from all of it.

Ramses: Hey, missed you before class this morning. What's up?

A text from Ramses came in the middle of fourth period, and after checking to make sure my algebra teacher was at the white board, I eased my phone out from under my notebook.

Me: Sorry. I forgot I had a meeting with my history teacher. Totally crapping out in that class.

That was true, but so not the reason for the avoidance. I hadn't wanted the confrontation with Ramses. We'd have to be fake again, and I just wanted to put that off for a second more. I really didn't know how to bring up that I was having second thoughts about the whole thing. I mean, he may have had his own reasons for joining the Court, but my sister and I had definitely been the catalyst for it. He'd invested so much, sat out in the middle of the frickin' woods in his boxers for that ring on his finger, so yeah. I didn't know how to tell him I was reconsidering some things.

Ramses: Ah. Well, no problem. Just missed seeing you.

I swallowed.

Me: You dork. You did not.

Ramses: So did! All that expensive shit at my house is boring without others like yourself to mooch off it with me.

Happy for a laugh for once, I smiled, covering my mouth since I was still in class.

Ramses: Speaking of. You totally ghosted my ass. What's up with that? Everything okay?

I had ghosted him, but not completely because I wanted to avoid him. I'd been involved with this new project regarding my sister, trying to figure out who she'd been dating, and honestly, that's where my head had been at completely.

Me: Just been busy. We'll talk. Later when I see you.

Ramses: K. K.

No sooner had he said it than the bell rang for lunch. I gathered my stuff and immediately headed for Kiki's locker. We usually met there, then met up with the others at lunch since her locker was right outside my fourth hour.

"You heard about Ramses, right?" the tall goddess said to me in passing. Seriously, she looked beautiful like every moment of the day. It was hard to believe she actually played sports and sweated. She pushed black strands out of her face. "Like the school is seriously freaking, and you missed it this morning."

"Missed what?" I asked, pushing the doors open to the lunchroom. We got inside, and all she had to do was point. I spotted Ramses at our usual table and he was actually sitting on top of it. His arms expanded wide, he looked like a frickin' mage telling a grandiose story. No doubt about his suspension, and I started to laugh until I realized how many people were at our table with him.

I laughed even less when I saw their fingers.

The boys had a shine on their right hands, king rings and the girls underneath their arms wore necklaces. They wore necklaces like mine and that symbol I still wore to keep up with appearances.

"What the fuck?" fell from my mouth, and it'd been loud enough over the chaos for Ramses and crew to notice me.

A loud and vibrant, "'Zona!" shouted my way, and immediately leaving the table, Ramses came over. He pounded Kiki's fist, allowing her to pass before coming to my side. She headed into the lunch line, and shocked, I just stood there.

"What the fuck is this?" I asked him, stunned to hell. Like seriously, half the lunch room was at our table.

He leaned in. "Frickin' craziness. Watch this shit." He waved and the crowd at the table hooted, pointing at him, and he pointed back. He hunkered down again. "I don't know. I just sat down and they all came over. This is wild."

But was it? Was it really? He'd gotten in a fight with who was the king of the school, a king whose own table was looking a little worse for wear. I noticed it quickly, panning to the place Royal, LJ, Knight, and Jax normally sat at. LJ, Knight, and Jax were still there, but their table was noticeably absent of people, both guys and girls.

I guess we picked up the slack.

There was seriously a circus going on at our table, and after Ramses waved at them again, he faced me.

"Play along," he said, taking my hand. Before all the drama of the fight and everything else, I'd been more than game to do that.

But now?

Now it felt weird, foreign, and the only reason I didn't let go was for appearances. I let Ramses guide me over to the table, everyone swarming me just like they had him. Through the chaos, I noticed LJ and Jax looking at me, us.

Knight hadn't even bothered to look.

He ate his sandwich to himself, doing his own thing as I was forced to sit down between Ramses and another Court-kept girl. Kiki had joined us at this point, and she, Shakira, and even Birdie were chatting it up with some Court guys across the table. The girls were getting cozy, getting used to this.

I settled in while conversation happened around me, smiling when nodded to and talking when prompted to do the same. My gaze fell on Ramses quite a few times during all of it, the storyteller, the mage everyone sat on the edge of their seats for just to hear his next words. It seemed Windsor Preparatory had a new kingpin.

It seemed they had a new Royal Prinze.

CHAPTER
NINETEEN

Royal

"I'll be right back." I paid the ride share driver in cash to wait, easier and unable to be tracked. The last thing I needed was my dad to know I hopped a plane.

Let alone I was on the other side of the country.

None of that was his business, and how I spent the duration of my suspension he couldn't give two shits about anyway. I'd already embarrassed him by getting kicked out of school, and he handed me my ass for it.

Those bruises finally starting to fade, I slid a dozen red roses off the seat. Shutting the door, I tucked them under my arm as I walked. I hadn't been here before, but I felt like I knew the area well. The guys had described it in detail, the pictures they showed me only helped. I easily navigated the cemetery.

I easily found my best friend.

A sock in the chest hurt less, the pain of *everything* coming to fruition. Standing here, I had to face reality. I had to face *her* and all my failures.

I couldn't do it…

My thoughts consumed me as my knees hit the ground, Paige's headstone right in front of me. They buried her next to her mom, *her mom* like it was her time to be buried. Neither of them should have been, all of it too fucking soon.

I put my hand on the stone, the rock hot from the California heat. I hadn't been out here for the internment of the ashes, telling myself it was for her. I'd been fighting and still was *for her* but I knew the truth now. I was weak. I failed her in every way, and I knew that just as well as I was on my knees now.

"I can't find it…" I retched over her stone, shaking. I pressed the roses into the dirt, touching my head against the stone. "I tried, Paige. I *tried*, but I can't fucking find it!"

I couldn't do it… The one thing I needed to do to justify everything I'd done and had been willing to do. I'd been all in, fighting from my core to bring about some fucking justice in this world, to bring some fucking justice to my friend…

To find out her truth.

But I couldn't even do that, *weak* and letting go of the roses, I reached into my pocket. I pulled out that dingy old handkerchief. One I'd let get dirty, one I'd let suffer through time to the point it was now. A quick tie and I had it around the roses, giving it back to her when I put the roses in front of her headstone. It belonged with her. It wasn't good enough for me and never had been.

"Are… Are you all right, young man?"

Words from my side, I wiped my eyes, getting my shit together when I faced a woman. She came up herself with a bundle of flowers in her hands, daisies, and I recognized her. I'd never met her before, but she'd been at Paige's reception.

I got to my feet before the middle-aged woman, one with dark hair and deep dark eyes that reminded me not of my friend but someone else.

The pain ripped raw again as I looked at her, and staring away, I stepped back from the stone.

"I'm fine," I said, a bald-faced fucking lie. I swallowed, tucking my hands into my pockets. "Just paying my respects."

The woman approached closer, looking so fucking close to December it really did hurt. I recalled the invitation to Paige's reception mentioning it was at her aunt's house and this woman looked so close to both Lindquist sisters this had to be her. Their aunt Celeste. She ventured slowly, but eventually, eased up and no longer looked at me like I was a freak. She crossed the rest of the grass over to me with her daisies in her arms, and my face must have healed up enough not to put her off. She stared right at me, her smile slight as she lowered the flowers.

"You knew Paige?" she asked, and I nodded. Her smiled lifted. "That's so nice you came to see her. The second this week."

"The second?" I questioned, standing back and letting her pay her respects. As it turned out, she had two sets of flowers. One bunch she placed on the headstone belonging to Paige and the other on Paige's mom's. The woman stared at that one a while, putting her hand on it like I had.

She nodded. "Yes, so nice. No one has come since the internment. No one but me." She put hands on both stones, running her palms along them. "I hate that they're together. I hate they're like this."

I hated so much more, none of this fair at all. Paige *shouldn't* have died. She…

Her aunt dampened her lips before looking up at me. "Are you from Maywood Heights too? The other woman was."

"Other woman?" I asked and she nodded again.

"So far to come, I thought." She faced the grave. "She stayed for hours."

My eyes narrowed. "What did she look like?"

"Tall, lovely…" She shook her head. "So many hours she was here."

So many hours… So many…

"Did she say her name?" My voice stiffened, hard as I waited, and when Paige's aunt shook her head, I found myself reaching into my pocket. I took out my phone, leaving.

"Young man?"

Her aunt called to me, but I was already making another call and walking away.

LJ picked up on the first ring.

"What's up?" he asked. "You're done already?"

He knew I'd flown here. All the guys knew, but what they didn't and *we didn't* was connecting someone to all this who hadn't been in the cards before. We had no reason really, other evidence leading us in another direction.

Maybe it was leading us in the ultimate direction.

"We need to meet up," I said. "I don't think just my dad's involved."

CHAPTER
TWENTY

December

"Hey. Royal's back," Birdie tossed at me before gym class. She backed down the hallway. "Just wanted to let you know."

I gazed up at the clock in the hall, minutes before I had to be across campus for my next class. I slammed my locker, heading instead in the opposite direction. Birdie probably thought to give me a heads-up for good reason. The last time Royal had been in these halls, he'd fought Ramses because of me.

I headed over toward his locker to find him, ignoring Jax's warning. Some time had passed since those moments at his house, and maybe, the two of us standing in front of each other could talk some of it over.

I could only hope.

I braved up, hoping to God he was alone and willing to talk to me *if* I found him. I knew where his locker was, so getting there was easy. Rounding the corner, I fully expected to find him with a shit-ton of people around him.

Imagine my surprise when I found him alone.

He was pulling books out of his locker, his uniform pristine this time. It was no longer ripped and tattered, his hair no longer messy, and as I got closer, he'd healed. His bruises were gone, and the ones under his eyes the same.

I knew because he looked at me.

He stared right at me, only the two of us in the hallway. He must have heard me, but as I got closer, he merely moved those green irises back to what he was doing. He continued to mess in his locker, and I chewed my lip.

"Hi," I said, the simplest thing to say when I got beside him.

A thick arm accompanied the grapple of a book from the top shelf. "What's up?"

The chill outside was less cold. I pushed arms around my front. "You're back."

"Seems that way." More chill, and I wanted to shake him, get him to open up… *do something*, but he just continued to fool around with his stuff.

I forced out a harsh breath. "I think we should talk. About some of the things you said?" He said so many things, confusing things, and I just needed some damn answers. "Royal—"

A locker slammed, and I blanched, Royal tossing his book bag on his back. He pushed a hand into his pocket, that green stare pinned directly on me. Royal and I had a few tense exchanges, ones where he'd wanted me to stay out of his way. But even in the past, it hadn't been this, though. He hadn't looked completely over me and something I said to him.

That was his look now, the boy taking the steps to move closer to me. He wet his lips. "Conversation?"

What the…

Thrown, I blinked wide. "Our conversation we had. You know… That last one?"

Again he passed it off, a fucking shoulder shrug this time.

"Gotta go. You probably should too. Probably shouldn't get into any more trouble around here. At least me."

He left me with nothing more than that before passing me, and my heart squeezing, I backed into his locker. I didn't watch him as he walked away from me, down the hallway and to his own classes. I couldn't.

I was having a hard time standing.

He was really doing this, shutting me out, and closing my eyes, I opened them only to almost run into someone. I hadn't expected Mira to be there, his girlfriend, Mira, let alone her death stare.

She gave that to me full on, her arms folded over her chest. Knowing I ran into her, I passed her a mumbled "sorry" before passing around her. With the fragile state I was currently in, I didn't feel like dealing with her too.

"I hope you don't think you're just going to walk past me like that," she said, causing me to stop. "You've been avoiding me like a little bitch, and I think you owe me the courtesy of at least a chat. Especially after getting my boyfriend suspended."

My jaw working, I forced myself to face this asshole. She was so in the wrong here it wasn't even funny. I shook my head. "I don't know what you're talking…"

So quickly she got into my face, so fucking quick. In a flash, she had an acrylic fingernail pointed in my direction, and it look all I had not to rip her finger away and snap it in two. I stood there, my patience tested, but not for long if she didn't back the hell up. "Mira, you seriously need to put some distance between us right now."

"*I* need to put some distance?" She put her finger down only to prop hands on her hips. "You need to put some distance between you and Royal. What do you think is going on between you two, and why in the entire fuck is he getting into fights with you in the middle?"

"I don't have time for this—"

She grabbed me. Like actually fucking grabbed me by the arm, and I swore to God I saw red. I swore to *God* it would be World War fucking three if she didn't get her hand off me right now.

"I could end him, you know?" Paused me, though, the words seething from Mira's ruby red lips. "I can and I will. I got something over on him, December. Something so terrible I wouldn't hesitate to let come out if only to keep him away from you."

I eyed her, my eyebrows narrowing. I started to question, but she let go of me.

"Stay away from my man," she said and, with that, fluffed her hair out. She headed in the opposite direction.

What the fuck?

CHAPTER
TWENTY-ONE

December

So Mira had something on Royal, did she? Of course she did, and suddenly it all made sense. Suddenly, *their relationship* made sense. It'd seemed to come out of nowhere when it happened. I'd seen them together at my sister's reception, something she'd definitely not been invited to attend, and the way it'd gone down had been so odd. He'd shut me out right after that, abandoned me and shipped me off to fucking Arizona, only for me to come back and him to tell me he needed her. Maybe he hadn't needed her really.

Maybe he had no choice.

Things were starting to click, but what wasn't were Royal's secrets and the dangers I may or may not be in knowing information about what happened that night with my sister. Whatever was going on, more questions were warranted, though, and previous plans seemed to be in the wrong direction. I needed to reanalyze how I was handling certain things, so the note from Ramses in English 8 couldn't have come at a better time. He'd tossed it right down my front, and I opened it.

Ramses: I hear Prinze is back. We probably should talk about some stuff.

I turned, his nod small. I watched him scribble down something again, and when I turned back, that note came down my front too.

Ramses: I also really do feel like you've been ghosting me. No jokes this time. We need to talk, 'Zona. What's going on?

What was going on was I was fucking confused, confused about how we started this semester and where we were going now. I was confused about Royal and both his feelings and mine. A lot was going on.

I scribbled down words.

Me: Let's talk at lunch. At the greenhouse.

Ramses and I had only gone out there that one time, the first time when he'd arrived at our school, and he'd been so candid with me. He told me who he was and why he was there, always honest from the beginning. He may have not gone into too many details surrounding that honesty, but he'd always told me the truth. I owed him that right.

We got out there in our coats and fully equipped with our lunches, Ramses opened the door for me. The heat from the greenhouse was heaven, and I had to say, it'd be nice to have an open conversation for once. I had been avoiding him, doing my own stuff behind the scenes like trying to find out more about my sister's ex-girlfriend. I still hadn't really found anything out about that, but I was hoping that wouldn't be forever. It'd also be nice to have lunch for once where half a dozen people I didn't know or cared about weren't sitting with me. Ramses was kind of popular before the whole Court thing, but now, with that king ring on his finger, he'd turned into god status. Everyone wanted a piece of him, to be around him just because he was in Court now. It was crazy, but that amount of power had been what we wanted. It'd help us open some doors, doors I'd pretty much been avoiding until this very moment.

"So what's going on?" he asked, passing me a pita chip. I noticed he started getting them through the lunch line especially for me. He always made sure to have some when we sat next to each other, no doubt just keeping up with the ruse. He was so much better at all this girlfriend/boyfriend stuff than me, a natural for him almost.

I took the chip. "I think we need to reconsider how we've been handling things."

"Okay." Taking the bag back, he ate a chip himself. "How so?"

I felt so guilty I hadn't told him any of the stuff about Royal, our conversation right after Royal had been suspended or what happened when I went to his house. Ramses had been more than honest and upfront with me than I'd ever been with him, and I pretty much felt like a shit friend because of that. He'd been doing so much for me, putting up with this lie *for me* basically. I sat near the koi pond. "I talked to Royal."

This had his dark eyebrows rising, and scarfing another chip, he took the all of two steps it took him to cross the greenhouse over to me with his long legs. He sat down with the bag. "You did?"

"Yeah, a few times actually. The latest was earlier today."

He ate in silence, and I couldn't get a read on him. He swallowed. "All right. So what does that mean? What did you guys talk about?"

Where did I start? I folded my arms. "Well, the first time was after the fight. Like right after. I cornered him, yelling at him about it. A lot of stuff was said, but it was short, so I decided to go talk to him. I went to his house not long after that."

"Wait. What?" He sat back. "'Zona, have you lost your

mind? He could be a serial killer. I mean, he basically is with the Route 80 thing."

"But that's the thing—I don't know if it's as simple as that. He pretty much told me the haze was my sister's idea. More to everything that night than we believed. It's basically what you said. We didn't have the whole story, so didn't know what to conclude."

"He told you the haze was your sister's idea?" he asked propping his elbows on his knees. "Like actually told you that and admitted it to you?"

"In so many words."

His eyes lifted toward the heavens. "'Zona…"

"Seriously, Ramses, I don't think what happened was necessarily his fault or the other guys'. He said he begged Paige not to."

"Why had he let her? No offense, December, but I don't remember your sister being a huge girl. He physically could have kept her from doing something."

"But could he have? Really? No offense, Ramses, but you don't know my sister. If she wanted to do something, she was going to do it. To hell with Royal or not."

"But why would she?" He dropped arms between his legs. "What would compel her to do something that crazy? A haze like that someone would want to make a statement, gain some clout against the brothers."

"Maybe that's why that one was so important. She was a girl, a girl who's trying to *be* Court and not kept, and from what I understand, she did have a reason."

"Which is?"

My jaw moved. "Revenge."

"Revenge?"

I nodded. "And Royal told me that too. That was the reason for the whole thing. She wanted to get someone back and do so with the power of the Court."

"Who?"

Thinking about previous investigations, I faced him. "I have my suspicions. But only that."

Ramses considered that, reaching into his bag and crunching on chips again. "And Prinze admitted all this to you? Openly?"

"Pretty much."

"And you believe him?" He now was almost angry and definitely judgmental from the way he stared at me. "Because he's dangerous, December. Obviously with what we know."

"With what we *think* we know, Ramses." I stood. "Royal is a lot of things, yes, but there's also so many things we don't know, *you* don't know."

Like how he had a heart, a huge heart, and showed it when he didn't think people were looking. I recalled the stuff he'd done for me in the past. Helping me with Hershey, saving me and Hershey at one point, and then the other things. He sent Knight to Arizona to watch over me, an action that ultimately kept something really bad from happening to me in the end. Thinking it over, Royal had done a multitude of things that, at the time, I hadn't understood, but maybe I was starting to now. This thing with Mira only helped support it, his possible obligation to her and pushing me away. What if he really was just with her because he had no choice? What if he broke things off *with me* because of that choice?

And then there was how he'd helped Ramses.

It was something Ramses would never know, as I didn't have the courage to tell him. Royal protected Ramses and had obviously done so for me.

"I think you know why, Em…"

He'd said that to me too, keeping Ramses from that other haze for me. Knowing that information may or may not hurt Ramses' pride, and I didn't want to make things worse. I'd kept all this from him, talked to Royal instead of him, when initially, we'd been in all this together. I didn't want to lose our friendship. It was something that was important to me and kept me out of a lot of hard times in the past.

Ramses sighed, his large shoulders sagging. Balling up the chip bag, he tossed it in the trash.

"What do you need from me, then?" he asked, surprising me. He really was that friend I believed, completely there for me even though I didn't deserve it. He didn't owe me anything.

Maybe that's what made him better than me.

I snuck a glance over. "You still wanna help?"

He shrugged. "I don't trust Prinze as far as I can throw him, but if you believe in him. I'll help you."

Relieved by that, I threw my arms around him, I think surprising us both. I'd hugged him before when I thought he was dying. And really, that time hadn't counted because I was just trying to get him warm.

Unlike that last time, he was able to hug back, his arms no longer bound. Laughing, he pulled away, and when he looked at me, he was smiling. "All right, but I didn't say this wouldn't come without a cost. You'd owe me. Seriously, I can't stand that guy."

Chuckling, I sat back. "Okay, how would I owe you?"

This got that Ramses to grin. He crossed his legs at the knee. "Nothing too big. Just a break from our double lives for a night. You game?"

Was I game? Seriously, I'd be owing him. I laughed. "Duh. What do you want to do?"

The alarm sounding the end of lunch flooded over the campus, and after tossing away the rest of the trash, we got our coats back on.

"It's really nothing major," he said, handing me mine. "Just dinner."

"Dinner?"

"Yeah, um... with my family."

That gave me pause, but before I could protest, he put up his hands. "Okay, so it's so not really a thing."

"How is it not a thing, and how is *that* a break from our double lives?"

"It honestly is. It's just family dinner. It happens once a month, and it's my mom's way of making us all check in with each other. My dad's like never around because of his job, and this will be the first time I basically have to face him since the fight and all that suspension stuff. Because of that, it'll be awkward as hell, and I need a buffer—you."

"But don't they know we're dating? Your mom and dad?"

He snorted. "Please. My dad is running the town. Doesn't get in my business, and my mom does her own thing too. It'd be a short dinner, and they probably won't even talk to us. My dad invites some of his staff too because, you know, *they're* family."

He sounded more than annoyed by that last bit, and though I sympathized with him, I was still skeptical. Seeing this, he got on his knees and actually grabbed my hands.

"Please. Please. *Please*. You'd be doing me a huge favor. I can't take another one of my dad's lectures. He seriously handed it to me when we left the school. Don't make me go through that again."

He popped out a lip, and I rolled my eyes. "You're an idiot."

"Yes, and a desperate idiot. Please help me. I'm helping you."

He was helping me, and ultimately, that had me nodding. He got up off his knees, hugging me now.

"Thank you," he said, and I guess I had another objective.

What did I wear when having dinner with the mayor and his wife?

CHAPTER
TWENTY-TWO

December

Ramses picked me up for family dinner later that evening, and I think the only reason I wasn't nervous about it was because he said we wouldn't have to fake tonight. According to him, his dad and mom had other priorities outside of the "little affairs" of himself, his words not mine, but I could imagine that was true. His dad was the frickin' mayor, and despite coming and going from his house a few times, I'd managed not to meet Mayor Mallick himself. He was always out of town or working, the same with his mom. She had a few businesses around the city, I guess, and seemed just as powerful as Royal's family if not more. Royal's family may have been in jewelry and banking, but Rameses's, well, they were on another level.

Ramses pulled through the gates of his family's mansion, and though I wasn't so much nervous, I did have reservations. I stopped him just as we pulled into a five-car garage.

"Principal Hastings won't be here tonight, right?" I asked, unstrapping myself. I had no problem with our headmaster, but eating with him was just too weird. I was still trying to get over the fact that Ramses was actually related to the guy, and he chuckled upon getting out of the car.

He came around his Mercedes, opening the door. "Don't worry about that. Uncle Leo never comes to these things. I think he has issues going to things where he has no control."

Though relieved, I nearly cringed, then shivered at him referring to my headmaster as his uncle. Ick. I didn't know what it was about it, but really, that freaked me the fuck out. I had a friend in middle school once whose mom was our homeroom teacher, and that was just too close for comfort. If it wasn't bad enough we had to see our teachers at school all day, then come home to them too? Just… yuck.

Anyway, after that was all off the table, Ramses led us through the garage and inside. I tried not to gawk over the various luxury vehicles that made the ones in Jax's garage look like Tinker Toys. This was just the town I lived in and the people around me, and I needed to get used to the fact. Ramses pushed open the door to delightful smells, and after saying hello to the kitchen staff, he led me from a room filled with pastries and cooking delectables into the hall. He grabbed my coat from me there, grinning when he opened the closet.

"And don't worry. The cooks have assured me they made something special for you to eat," he said, putting my coat in before taking off his own. His broad shoulders and long torso were in a thick wool sweater, an outline to a svelte but muscular frame. He also wore tan dress pants and suede shoes, and seeing that, I felt severely underdressed. I'd worn jeans and a nice top.

What were you thinking?

I was *thinking* I trusted the bastard who told me this dinner was going to be casual. After lunch today, I'd texted Ramses about what I should wear tonight, and not only had he passed it off, he'd assured me this dinner was totally casual.

It wasn't totally casual, judging by what he wore, and I hit him.

"Hey. What—"

I pointed to my jeans. "Okay, I'm completely under-dressed. Why did you tell me this thing was going to be casual?"

Ramses passed a glance to me, chuckling before rolling his eyes. "You look fine, 'Zona. Always do."

My face shot up a few degrees when he said that. Mostly because I knew he meant it. Ramses always told things like they were and had confidence about it I'd die for. He was secure in himself and didn't care about who knew that.

Wishing he could pass me some of that, I let him put my coat away despite wanting to keep it on. After, he framed himself. "Want me to go change so we look like gutter trash together?"

It took all I had not to throw him into the pretty walls of his house and run out of this bitch like there was no tomorrow. I'd admit. I tried to evade when I turned, but too quick, he got me by the arm.

"I'm just joking. You look *fine*," he emphasized again, laughing. "Anyway, no one is going to even be looking at you. My dad basically works through these dinners with his staff."

Something he'd pretty much said before but still.

I tugged on my shirt. "Fine."

He tilted his head. "Anyway, ready to go do this?"

Not really. Especially considering how I looked, but I'd get past it, letting Ramses throw his long reach around me. He led us out of the coat hall and into another, this place seriously a manor with how big it was. I'd only seen so much of it in the times I'd been here. When Birdie, the others, and I were usually here, we tended to stay to Ramses' section of the house and his game room, of course, in the basement.

"Oh, and I asked around about your sister's ex," he said, dropping his arm and putting his hand on a doorknob. "Haven't heard anything yet, but I'm sure we will."

The fact I hadn't bothered to ask the new king of Windsor Prep sooner to inquire about who my sister had been seeing before she died floored me. I'd been so quick to try to do this on my own when I clearly had friends.

I started to thank him when I was accosted from the front by, frankly, an amazing-smelling blond woman. She grabbed me, hugging the crap out of me.

"Oh my goodness. Oh my goodness. She's here. Why didn't you tell me, darling?" Yeah, she smelled good but was also gorgeous. Glittery green eyes stared down at me when the woman pulled back. And when I say stared down at me I meant it. The woman was easily over six feet tall and even bigger than my basketball-playing friends.

Standing next to the woman, Ramses' height was put to the test, but he still had a few inches on her. He merely chuckled while she accosted me. "Ma, let her go, please."

Ah, yes, his mom. I remembered seeing her at his family's Christmas party but only from a distance. I recalled her being glamorous then, but standing there in a shimmering gold top with mid-rise pants and pumps, I reevaluated my fashion choices again. Standing next to each other, Ramses and his mom looked like a fucking Christmas card, and then here I was. Yeah, looking like gutter trash.

She grabbed him. "Oh, Ramses. She's so adorable. So nice you have a little girlfriend."

Uh…

Ramses and I exchanged a glance, his eyes just as bugged out as I felt mine were in that moment.

What the fuck?

I shot Ramses a look, to which he responded with a frazzled, "I don't know." He mouthed it beside his mom, but when she grabbed me again, I couldn't say anything.

"Now, tell me all about yourself, December." She patted my hand. "My son has been keeping everything about you under lock and key."

"Uh, not much to me." As Ramses was next to *me* now, I grabbed his arm, squeezing tight. I hoped to cut off his goddamn circulation, but I couldn't get much grip with his stupid fucking sweater. Maybe I had because in the end, he guided me away from his mom by *my* arm.

He released my death grip, bringing me in to stand casual beside him. "What's with the interrogation, Mom? December is only here for dinner." He said this with a chuckle, but I think maybe only I noticed it was dry.

It made his mom's smile only frickin' widen.

What the hell?

She really thought we were together, how or why I didn't know. Ramses wouldn't just sideline me with something like this. At least, I hoped he wouldn't. In any sense, the doorbell rang, and waving her hands, Mrs. Mallick backed away.

"That oughta be Liam and his wife," she said, prancing away in her little pumps. This woman was the epitome of the Real Housewives of Maywood Heights and did it so well. She lifted her hands. "I'm going to make sure they get in okay, and, Ramses, please take December to the dining room. So nice you have a date for once."

Ramses studied the floor, and I eyed him. His mom cleared herself, and no sooner had she left the hall than I punched him.

"Uh, ouch."

"You jerk." I shoved him again. "What the fuck?"

"Honestly, I have no idea how she knew. She never keeps up with me. Doesn't have time."

Well, she seemed to have the time now, and quick on my

feet, I reached into my turtleneck. I wore the Kept necklace as a backup just as case. Seeing this, Ramses' eyes widened.

"You wore that?"

I only took it off really in the shower. Ramses and I hadn't talked about what we were doing in regards to our fake relationship yet, so it's a good thing I did. Getting it adjusted, I threw my hair out over my shoulders. "I usually keep it on just in case."

Looking relieved by that, he pushed hands into his pockets. "Well, that's good. Good thinking."

"Does your dad think we're together too?" I'd hate to have to lie to the *mayor*, and Ramses raised a hand.

"Doubt it. But if he does, we'll play it off. I got you."

I hoped so, and opening the door, Ramses let us into the dining room, but really, it looked like a catalog feature for *Better Homes and Gardens*. Large white flowers on the table and chairs and tulle on the back of the chairs like this was a goddamn wedding. Then there was the spread, all kinds of frickin' food as white-gloved attendants stood against the walls in wait of assistance.

"*This* is family dinner?" Ramses pulled my chair out, and I sat down.

He sat beside me. "Mom gets really into it."

"Apparently."

A door behind us eased open, and Ramses' mom clicked in with a new arrival, a thirty-something man in a business suit. She introduced him to me as Liam, the mayor's chief of staff, and after I shook his hand, his mom seated him at the end of the table.

"Gets to sit next to the big man," Ramses edged in. "He's obviously not family, but might as well be. Dad sees him more than anyone else."

A bit of spite came with that comment, but another arrival came in, and we pulled apart. The woman was dazzling in her silver gown and immediately hugged Ramses' mom.

"Thanks for letting me use your hand lotion, Evelyn. It's just so dry outside right now." The woman rubbed her hands, then noticed me. Like stopped right in the conversation. I knew her too; I just didn't know *which one of her* I knew.

She and her sister were twins after all.

Either Mrs. Hastings or her sister stood in front of me right now. I assumed Mrs. Hastings since she was married to Ramses' uncle, but when Ramses' mom introduced her to me as Daisy, the wife of the mayor's chief of staff, Liam, that cleared everything up.

"Oh, we've met," Daisy said, her smile warm on me. She stood back. "I had no idea you'd be here tonight."

"Well, I think it's new," Ramses' mom edged in. "I believe they've just started dating. I heard from some of the girls downtown when I mentioned who Ramses said he'd be bringing to dinner tonight."

So apparently Ramses and I were the talk of the town. My eyes averted, and Ramses palmed his face.

"Mom, seriously?"

She waved him off. "Oh, you'll stop and let me gush. She's gorgeous, and you never bring any girls home."

"For good reason." Ramses' look was apologetic as he stared at me. "I'm sorry."

It was cool, but it wasn't. It was what it was and something we'd ultimately decided together so it wasn't his fault. We knew what we were getting into when we decided to pull this.

I just didn't know how big it'd get.

It was big, the whole room staring at us. Even the mayor's chief of staff, Liam, had his eyes in our direction. All focus on me, no one realized when the mayor came in, and I believed only I had because he stared right at me.

He stopped, an older man of maybe forty or fifty. He had a bronze shade to his skin, his hair a salt and pepper. He looked a lot like Ramses, but didn't. Obviously older. His family's attention on me, the mayor's eyes narrowed. "What's going on here?"

We all looked at him, Ramses' mom going over. She put a hand on his arm. "Darling, this is the friend Ramses brought. December Lindquist. She's his girlfriend."

She whispered that last bit, giggling, but the mayor didn't giggle. He frowned, and looking at Ramses, his thick, dark eyebrows narrowed only harder.

"Is that true?" Mayor Mallick asked. He panned to me. "Are you two dating?"

Ramses said nothing, his hand on his face. Dropping it with a sigh, he chose to nod, and his dad came over.

He put out a hand. "Nice to meet you."

Immediately standing, I put a hand in his. "Nice to meet you, sir."

I didn't know whether I should call him "sire" or even "your majesty." All in all, I felt neither was appropriate, and we all sat but only after the mayor did. He was royalty in his own house, and placing his hands on the table, his attention transferred to me. Liam immediately began chatting off his ear, business things from what I heard, but the mayor wasn't hearing any of it. He kept looking at me, and feeling awkward, I stared at Ramses.

"Does your dad not like me or…"

"It's time for grace." The mayor's proclamation cut my question off, his hands out. Ramses took one while Liam took the other, his wife Daisy across from me holding her husband's hand. Evelyn sat on the opposite end of the table, and together, everyone sat quietly while the mayor said a few words. After, the staff came in, plating salads and assisting. I started to go for mine, but once again, I noticed the mayor. He was talking to Liam but kept looking over at me, and I assumed because Ramses really didn't bring any girls around here. Eventually, the mayor noticed *me* noticing, and waving Liam off, he shifted complete focus to me.

"There's always time for business, Liam," he said to him, then folded his hands over his salad. "But it isn't every day my son brings a girl home. Please, December. Tells us about yourself—"

"Dad, come on." Ramses sat back. "When have you ever cared about who I'm dating?"

"Since now, and you don't talk." He directed a finger. "Not right now, and what you've been getting into. You've been disgracing this family, so it's the least you can do to let me talk in my own house."

Ramses' nostrils flared, but his dad must have had something there, so he stopped talking. Ramses pulled his napkin off his lap, apparently no appetite when he placed it on the table. The room suddenly silent, everyone's eyes averted. Everyone but the mayor's.

He had his focus on me and continued to keep it. He opened his hands. "Now, December. Please. Tells us everything about you. Tell us what my son apparently wanted to keep quiet."

Dishes clanked awkwardly around me, all but Ramses', who had so much heat coming off him I thought he might punch a wall. I might just punch him after this was over.

So much for a night off faking.

CHAPTER
TWENTY-THREE

Ramses

I pressed my head back to the seat of my Mercedes, barely able to look at December let alone talk to her. I folded a hand over my eyes. "God, I'm so sorry."

My dad interrogated her tonight, asked her everything about herself short of her blood type. At one point, I thought he'd actually ask to get a test of that.

"Just want to know who you've been seeing, son," he'd stated, all nonchalant about it like he wasn't all up in her business. *"Nothing wrong with knowing how our son is spending his time…"*

Only except for the fact that he'd never given a shit about it before. But now, it seemed to be open season on, of all people, my fake girlfriend. The kicker had been when he had asked about December's college plans—newsflash, she hadn't had any. Nothing wrong with that, but when Dad had found *that* out, he'd asked if she would be staying in town, and once she'd said yes, he'd asked her why, *why* like that was any of his business at all. He seriously couldn't grasp the concept why someone might want to take both a break from life and/or school and just *be*.

Especially someone who'd been through as much as December.

The whole thing had been a disaster, seriously messed up. I begged help from my mom and got zip, nada, and nothing. She wanted to know stuff too, like friggin' everything, and was there along for it with my dad. By the end, I had to peel them away from her, the both of them completely out of line.

Maybe if I'd brought more girls over, things wouldn't be that way. But after all that shit that went down with my last relationship, my girlfriend cheating on me in AZ, I'd been gun-shy to get invested in anything, let alone take someone home. December got to pay for that tonight, and I turned my head, looking at her. Her eyes were currently out the window, the pair of us parked in her dad's driveway. We'd been sitting there for several minutes. I sighed. "He's seriously never like that. I don't know what got into him, my mom."

Things had been getting into him since the fight. He laid into me after we got in the car, like seriously lost his shit. I hadn't understood it. He never cared before.

I guess he did now, this stupid fucking ring on my finger. He was proud of me or some shit, invested. I guess, in the end, I'd done that to myself.

December didn't say anything, playing with the necklace around her neck. It was the necklace I'd given her. She faced me. "It wasn't so bad."

She was being nice as hell right now and definitely not what she should be. I told her I'd have her back tonight. I frowned. "My dad was being an ass. He's never leaned in so hard before. I think it's this ring. It's doing something to him."

I held it up for emphasis, the influence of *this*, and that had to be what tonight was about. I existed to my dad now that I'd earned my way into the Court. I existed where I hadn't before, legacy.

December continued to play with her necklace, and noticing me staring at her, she let it go. "I guess it's a good thing I wore this, then. I don't usually take it off."

She didn't? Never? I watched her play with it more. I'd had serious reservations when I gave it to her initially. I knew she agreed with the plan in the end, but giving her that necklace normally meant something.

And she never took it off?

I guess I was glad she'd thought to be prepared when I hadn't. I let her go to the wolves tonight, and if it hadn't been for my dad's pushy-ass chief of staff, Liam, bugging him about politics from time to time during the interrogation, Dad would have been all over her all of the night and not just some of it. "I should have protected you. He's ridiculous."

She raised a shoulder, her dark hair sliding over her shoulder. The fact that she'd been so uneasy about the way she looked tonight blew me away. I'd told her once she was a bombshell, and I didn't retract from those thoughts. December didn't even have to try like most girls, just be herself.

Sitting back and away from those thoughts, I watched her face forward. She sighed. "At least with him you know what you're getting into. My dad is just—" She paused, shaking her head. "My dad is so hot and cold. He asked me like a million questions tonight before you came to pick me up. Questioning me like he cares and so phony about it."

"Phony?" I asked.

"He doesn't care about me, not really. I think he cares about you and the fact I'm hanging out with you, the mayor's son." She folded arms over her fluffy coat. "I haven't told him about our fake relationship, but it wouldn't surprise me if he'd heard something like your mom."

In this town, I wouldn't be surprised either. I sighed.

December frowned. "Needless to say, he was pushing me to go out the door tonight. I just wished he'd care about me. Like actually care."

That last bit I barely heard. She whispered it, and I turned my head on the seat again, just watching her. There was so much trauma between us both, hurt inflicted by both our fathers. I'd learned to deal with mine head on after dear old Dad shipped me away to boarding school. That's just how things were in my world and this crazy-ass town, but I hated she had to deal with her own shit. Things were so much worse for her. She'd lost her sister, which made me hate what we'd been doing together even more. Every day we continued the ruse of our relationship, it made her relive the hurt of her sister and the reasons behind it. It was one of the biggest regrets I had for even suggesting the whole plan of a fake relationship to her in the first place.

Well, one of a few.

Thinking about some new information I'd received today, I stared at December. I had made a lot of selfish decisions when it came to her. I'd put myself and revenge first, but all that got me was this. A girl and a fake relationship.

My chest caved. "Maybe he does care," I said, being honest. "You never know until you let him."

Her dark lashes flashed up, her head shaking. "I don't have time for it. Time for him."

And I guess that would be up to her, but I still thought she should try. We didn't all have fathers that actually cared, ones whose care wasn't tied to ambition or motive. My dad may have expressed interest in me now, but he never had before. Not until I'd done what he wanted and how. I folded my arms. "I get what you're saying. And what you choose to do is entirely up to you. When it comes to my dad, I know what I'm getting. I know he's an elitist snob who only gives a shit if it suits him, so if some reason out of the blue he gave any inclination or even an iota of thought about me that came with zero ties or personal objectives… If he showed he actually cared and gave effort to show that care?" I laughed. "I'd be thanking my lucky stars for a chance to do something with that."

I let all that slip out, and I knew the moment I captured that dark gaze of hers, her irises so big and bright like the stars above. They were a light in this town that wasn't deserved, not by anyone. Even me.

The glow of it far too hot, I faced away, tapping my steering wheel.

"I have an idea." I started up the car, my Mercedes humming. "Strap in. Neither of us want to go home, so let's do part two of this night."

"Part two?" she asked, and though she questioned me, she sat up, belting in. "I was barely able to get through part one."

Something I was about to correct now. The both of us strapped in, I used the rearview camera to back down the driveway. In the street, I placed the car in drive, then pulled away. I promised her a night of no faking.

Especially since this was most likely our last night.

CHAPTER
TWENTY-FOUR

December

Ramses had been way too secretive, but for whatever reason,
that made me more excited than scared. It put me at ease in a
way it shouldn't when everything in my life was all over the
place. The stuff with his dad seriously hadn't been that bad.
Compared to the other crap I'd been dealing with in my life,
it'd been a breath of fresh air and a night gratefully away
from my own home and under my dad's eye. Ramses allowed
me to escape tonight, and that continued when we drove out
into the boonies. I didn't really recognize the route or
anything else with all the farmland and it being so dark, but
when we pulled toward a familiar building in the night, I
sat up.

I recognized Maywood Heights Community Recreation
Center well. I worked there for all of a minute. It'd been
another one of my dad's heavy-handed maneuvers he made
when I first arrived here. He had me so hard under his thumb
initially, got me a job I didn't want to do and under people I
didn't want to be under. LJ had been my manager of all

people, worked me to the bone, and for whatever reason, Ramses was pulling us into the parking lot.

The wide lot was basically empty, a far cry from the days I worked there. People were coming in and out of the place like someone cried fire it'd been so busy. Parking right up front, Ramses turned off his car, then got out his cell phone.

"What are we doing?" I asked, this guy being so secretive. He merely grinned before putting away his phone. Going outside, he opened my door for me, and I eyed him.

He rolled his. "Just go with me on this, 'Zona. I promised you a night off from our double life, so will you let me give it?"

Still unsure, I sat there for a moment. I think the only reason I got out in the end was because he was outside with no coat on, still in his sweater and dress pants. He probably thought he was just going to drop me off real quick and then come home. I got out. "Okay. I'm out, so what's going on? Why are we here?"

He grinned again, closing the door before guiding me to follow him. He pushed hands into his pockets during his strides. "A guy in there owes me one. I'm going to collect, and you are going to reap the spoils of those benefits."

Ramses was seriously talking like a mob boss right now, but I guess I trusted him. I had to take two steps for every one of his, and when we got to the doors, they were surprisingly unlocked. I assumed the place was closed with the lot so empty, and escaping the chill, I realized they were starting to close down for the night. People in familiar red uniform shirts were sweeping, cleaning up, and passing them, I grabbed Ramses' arm. "The guy who owes you isn't LJ, is it?"

Like stated, I'd worked here and worked with him for a time. I highly doubted with how things had gone with Royal he'd want to see me, and shaking his head of rogue curls, Ramses stared down at me.

"No, and come on, 'Zona. You wanna ruin the surprise?"

He flashed his big ole eyes at me with a pout, seriously looking like Hershey on her best cutesy days.

Lifting my eyes to the heavens, I let him take me into the crystal palace that was the community rec center. Like all things in this town it was flashy and exuberantly grandiose. It had a couple levels, and though I'd cleaned most of it during my time there, I hadn't been to where Ramses was taking me. He opened a door, and crisp air made me happy I still wore my coat. His surprise turned out to be the ice-skating rink, and when we went over to the wall, no one was out on the ice. Only a clear, flawless sheet was out there now, ready for the next set of skaters, and I looked at Ramses.

"An ice rink?" I questioned, eyeing him. "This is your surprise?"

Chuckling, Ramses shifted and lounged against the rink's barricade. "Not an ice rink, 'Zona. Ice-skating? Ever heard of it?"

I shoved him a little. "Of course I have, but we can't skate. Clearly, the rec center is about to close."

"Not for us. We have the place for the next hour. I took lessons here as a kid. The guy who runs the Zamboni I'm cool with."

As if he knew, a guy came in across the ice, waving at Ramses and asking if he needed anything. Ramses denied the help, waving his friend off, and when Ramses turned around, he clasped his hands together. He nudged me with his shoulder. "What do you say? I seriously need to make up for what happened tonight. Please. Please. *Please.*"

He begged me once again, but before he could get on his knees this time, I got a hold of his arm.

"I don't know how to skate," I confessed, all of this completely a bad idea, and not only did that not phase Ramses, he put out his hand. He put it out for mine, waiting.

"You won't have to," he said, gripping my hand when I allowed him to take it. He smiled. "You have me."

I did have him, had him this whole time, and I hadn't forgotten that. Ramses had been there in moments when no one else had, even out in Arizona when I'd been more than sketchy and given him every reason not to trust me. Even still, he'd been by my side, and when we finally got out on the ice, the same.

"Now, take small steps, 'Zona. Small steps," he coached, already out there himself. He looked like an Olympian skater with his easy glide on the ice. He even took it one further and did a few turns before skating back to me.

I currently gripped the wall like a lifeline, shaking my head. "Uh…"

"Oh, stop. Come on. You won't fall. I won't let you."

I gave him my hands, easier since I'd taken off my gloves. I'd done the same with my coat too since it wasn't as cold in here as I'd believed it was when we first came in.

I took baby steps, looking as awkward as a baby deer on new legs. I paid more attention to that than my own feet, feeling stupid, and Ramses tugged at my hands.

"Look at me," he said, making it easy to. He was so focused on me, everything about me in his eyes. He wouldn't let me fall, bracing my hands with a smile. "Good. You're doing it."

I was, standing up even. From somewhere holiday tunes started to seep into the rink, and Ramses had a good chuckle at that.

"Probably the last time they're going to get to do that for a while," he said, acknowledging the music. Meshing our hands, he guided me close and kept me upright. "No one wants to hear Christmas music after December."

I nudged him since I did like Christmas music after December and to my ultimate regret. I stumbled, taking him down with me, but not only did he catch himself, he caught me.

He braced me, chuckling as we both hovered over the ice.

"Hey, that's cheating," he said. "Trying to make me drop you."

I wasn't trying to make him drop anything, what I'd done stupid.

Kind of like this moment.

I knew because, when he tugged me toward him, I didn't pull away. At least not at first. I let him close his eyes and even brush our noses together. *I let him get that close* because things were easier with him. There was no heartache, no work, and that was easier. Being with Ramses Mallick would be the best thing for me…

So why did I push a hand between us?

His breath clouded the air when he opened his eyes, and righting me, he just held my hands. He didn't say a word, just looked at me.

"It's not me," he eventually said, staring away. He put space between us, and when he started to skate, I let him guide me away. He got quickly to the side of the ice, and after helping me back on stable ground, we sat together on the benches.

The silence deafened between us, me feeling guilt for pushing him away and whatever was going on inside his head.

"It's not you?" I asked, referencing what he'd said, and he nodded.

"It's not. Never has been," he said, glancing at me with a little smile. It didn't quite reach his eyes. "Never has been, has it?"

It took me a second, a harsh one, to realize what he was saying. Ultimately, I couldn't admit the answer to his question, though. I didn't want to hurt him, nor did I want to be foolish myself. Wanting to be with anyone but him was illogical. He was perfect, more than. Ramses had his flaws, yes, but so did anyone. He was a good person, made me laugh.

I gripped arms around my body, really fucking stupid. I

made myself think things were a certain way between us, probably ignored things a time or two when I shouldn't have.

You idiot.

I sighed. "Ramses…"

Instead of letting me talk, he reached into his pocket, pulling out his phone. He scrolled until he came across something.

"I want you to see something," he said, turning his phone over. "You need to see something."

I didn't understand what I was being shown at first, two columns on a sheet of paper. It was a picture of a sheet of paper, the first column with a few dozen tally lines. The other had only four. I shook my head. "What am I looking at?"

"All the people who hate me," he said, his laugh cynical when he said it. He pointed a finger. "You're looking at a vote, two options for hazes proposed by the membership. Column two is the haze you ultimately found me at, me shivering my shit down in the woods. The first column, the first option, is something else."

I panned, facing him.

His eyebrows narrowed. "They basically were going to whip me, hand my ass to me pretty hard. The first column is that whipping. I mean, I thought I pissed people off pretty bad with who I was back in the day, but really, these guys hated my ass."

The first column had all the votes, all but the four on the other side. But from what I knew about what went down that night, this vote I was seeing now didn't make sense.

I gave him back the phone. "How did you find this?"

He took the phone. "I found out today when I was asking about your sister. We were in the locker room, real candid talk and just chewing the fat. I guess I was trying to warm some of the guys up before asking, and this slipped out by one of them, this and what they were going to do to me."

"What they were going to do?"

Ramses messed with the phone again. He scrolled until he found another picture, another set of columns and a new vote. This time all the votes were on the other side, not the first column. His lips parted. "I honestly didn't believe it when they told me who fought for me. Who challenged that vote." He scrolled the phone again. "But maybe I do now."

He showed me that picture again, those four votes on the other side. They were obviously anonymous, but I didn't need to ask who those votes were. I'd been told personally by the person who changed the vote himself.

My heart raced.

Ramses sat back. "I have a feeling that change had less to do with me and more to do with you, 'Zona," he said, his smile small. "Those votes are Prinze, Knight Reed, Lance Johnson, and Jaxen Ambrose."

I knew they were, how much I did. I squeezed my hands together. "Royal told me he got the vote to change. It was the day you got suspended. I let in on him about what he did to you, and it came out. I wanted to tell you. I just..." I didn't know what to say and definitely didn't want his pride hurt. I shook my head. "It was a lot that day."

It was... still a lot, all these emotions. All this information I didn't know what to do anything with. I just knew I felt something for Royal, and it was something so strong it scared me. I didn't want him like this, all this *stuff* that was happening around us. I guess, in the end, I didn't have a choice. The heart wanted what it wanted...

And I wanted him.

Ramses whistled after what I said, and I felt really bad for keeping something about him from him. I frowned. "I really didn't want to keep all this from you..."

"It's not that." He waved a hand. "It's just Prinze has just been so caviler about telling you about Court stuff. Telling you where to find me out in the woods? This? Really, 'Zona. Anything he tells about Court business or the hazing process comes with a hell of a risk. I only did because I didn't give a fuck and we had a plan."

He mentioned that before, a code. He'd said there'd be consequences for information discussed with those on the outside.

"What exactly are the consequences of that?" I asked. "For telling me those things and if someone found out?"

He shrugged. "Only he would know. I haven't heard anything. But maybe he got away with the spill of information. It's possible."

Sure, it was, but what if he hadn't? What if he'd been punished for doing nothing but telling me the truth?

My chest caved even more, and when Ramses rubbed my shoulder, I gazed up.

He smiled. "You should go to him, figure this out?" He shook his head. "That guy loathes my ass, so if he's willing to fight for me, put all that past him for the sake of someone else…"

I swallowed.

"I still stand by what I said about him," he stated. "The Court and all this hazing stuff is bullshit, and though I'm acknowledging he's definitely not perfect, I think in the end, if it's not me… well, I'm glad it's him."

He was glad it's him.

I closed my eyes. I was glad it was him too.

shadow in the corner of my eye. I recalled failing to enable the security codes before showering.

Playing it cool and pretending I hadn't noticed, I stepped over to my desk drawer, sliding it open, but not to grab my phone and call the cops...

I got my hand around the nine millimeter, the gun I'd be using in the near future. I didn't think it'd be needed quite so soon.

I braced the weight of it, ready to end this now, whoever it was in my room.

"Royal?"

The gun slid back into the desk immediately, and when I whipped around, a girl was slipping into my room from behind curtains. She'd climbed a goddamn level to get up here, had to have scaled a tree on the outside. There was no ladder or vinery to climb below.

Em...

I recognized her before she'd even fully gotten out of the curtains, her beauty not able to be masked by any distraction or shadows. She stood out from it all, my little ounce of hope.

My little ounce of light.

She kept me on the right side of the darkness even now, a distraction for me, which was one of the biggest reasons I'd pushed her away yet again at school. I couldn't have her keeping me from what I needed to do in the end.

So why did I go to her?

We met in the middle of my bedroom, my hand on my towel while I watched her. She watched me too, the pair of us drinking each other in like we hadn't had a fucking taste of anything in days.

"Why are you here?" I asked her, hating her for being here. She couldn't be here, would mess things up, but even still, I let her approach. Her fucking flowery smell consumed my lungs, choking me because I couldn't have it and her.

How much I wanted her, the girl a goddess and everything I should have ever stayed away from. Even from the beginning of all this.

Dark eyes studied me in a dimly lit room, pink lips pouting and perfect. She wet them before crossing even more into my space.

She touched me.

My face at first, both hands, and they felt like such fucking heaven I wanted to melt beneath her. I wanted to worship her, beg her for her forgiveness. I wanted to beg her for hurting her and doing what I felt I had to do.

Her hands stopped around my eyes, one eye as she placed fingers beneath. Those scars had faded, but the deeper ones lingered beneath.

"Did he hit you?" she asked, her beautiful face cringing. "Did he hit you the day of the fight because of me?"

How could she even know that? That pretty much every strike that came from my dad lately had been because of things I'd done in connection to her. They weren't her fault, though. Choices *I* had made and not her.

I nodded because she asked me a question, but only that. I'd stood by what I had done and didn't regret it. I'd do anything for her.

Her touches continued on, and it started to hurt but not physically. Mentally and emotionally, it pained me to the point of explosion. I couldn't have her, too much at stake.

"Stop," I rasped, but leaned into every one of her touches, telling her the exact opposite of what I said. She knew what I wanted, no mystery between us. Even still, I fought it, eventually pulling her back by her shoulders…

Only to ultimately tug her closer.

I grabbed her by the back of her neck, releasing my towel and pressing my body up against hers. She gasped in response, her breath stolen away, and I picked her up, wrapping her legs around me.

"Em…" I pressed her down on my bed, leaning myself

into her. I fucking shuddered on top of her like I'd never touched a girl before.

She kissed me, breathing life into me with every one of her soft kisses. She didn't just take my mouth but my cheeks and my neck. I groaned for lack of impatience, immediately unzipping her coat and pulling it off her.

I threw it, her body so curvy and perfect even with her clothes on. I pressed my face between her breasts, breathing her in through her sweater.

"Why are you here?" I rasped, bunching her shirt up, then taking it off. I kissed her right between that supple valley, her bra lace and chest beautiful. "Why?"

She was ruining this for me, ruining *everything*. I couldn't be who I had to be with her in my life. I couldn't do what I had to do. She kept me from crossing a line I needed to cross, and I couldn't allow that.

I came up, brushing her nose, and she stopped me, her hands sliding across my face, then through my hair like fucking heaven.

"I want to be, Royal," she said, trembling too, and then she made me look at her, studying me almost in awe. She looked at me like I wasn't a monster.

She looked at me like I had a soul.

Pulling me down, she parted my lips, sighing hard into the kiss. "I love you," she said, then again and *again.* "I love you."

She loved me, my insides caving the rest of the way. I thought I'd travel into the depths...

Surprised when the other side turned into light.

So much clarity hit me, so many things coming into full circle. There was me and this girl, and that was damn everything.

I braced her, kissing everything away, my pain, my suffering. It all lessened with every kiss and taste.

"I fucking love you," I admitted to her, the truth for so

long. It was all before me like fucking reality. I loved her, and I'd loved her for so long. I gripped her to me. "I love you, Em."

She trembled once again, her bra strap sliding beneath my fingers. I pulled it away, kissing her right there on her shoulder.

She grabbed my hips in response, pressing me into her, so hard where she was soft. I had to feel her, unfastening her jeans and sliding them down her perfect legs. I kissed every ounce of skin I could find, tasted flesh even down to her toes. I needed her so much.

"Royal..." She gripped the sheets, her head back into my bed. She couldn't remain still, wriggling beneath me while I made sure not to miss any piece of her. I wanted every piece. I wanted every jagged edge. It made me not think about mine.

I delved a tongue into her belly button, sliding fingers into the side of her panties. I pulled them down as I released her breasts, skin on skin, flesh on flesh when I tossed the bra to the floor.

She called out, my hand on supple skin when I squeezed her breast. Her legs went up when I pulled her panties off, burying my face into her hair while I simply touched her, kissed her.

"Please," she begged, her legs easing apart, for me. "Please..."

I reached into my desk again, for protection this time. I got it around myself before taking her hands.

She let me, both of her tiny wrists gathered in one strong grip. I lifted them above her, her entire body flush and perfect. Pinning her, I placed my weight on her, being so careful. I didn't want to hurt her.

I eased myself inside her, both of us crying out. I couldn't even move at fucking first, all of it too much. Besides what happened at the beginning of term, I hadn't been with anyone else, and during that I hadn't felt anything. I'd had to get myself completely wasted and high to even do it. I had to numb myself so I wouldn't feel it.

I felt this, every bit of her as I pumped inside her. She braced me, telling me things. She said she loved me, how she needed me.

"I need you." I hated to admit it, feeling it made me weak. This girl was my Kryptonite, always had been.

Taking both of her hands now, I picked up, the pair of us creating a rhythm. I didn't take from her, refused. I'd fucking die first.

December's ankles crossed behind my back, making me move faster, driving harder. I gave her what she wanted and what I needed, this and every piece of her.

I kissed the inside of her arm, patient when she peaked first. I breathed kisses on her until I found that point myself, leaning so hard into it I thought I was literally falling. I couldn't catch myself, gratefully succumbing to the wave.

Spent, I allowed my weight to fall on her, releasing her arms above only to wrap them around my neck. As stupid as it was, I wanted her to hold me.

I wanted her to never let me go.

CHAPTER
TWENTY-SIX

December

Warm lips pressed against my back, and I closed my eyes. I stayed the night.

He let me stay the night.

Royal hadn't pushed me away. If anything, he wouldn't let me go away. He held me all night and this morning, when I woke up, his lips were on my skin. He held me close, absorbing his heat into me.

"I want to know everything," I said.

He stopped kissing, but only long enough to pull back my hair. He touched teeth down in my shoulder, biting me a little.

"Em…" he sighed, and I turned around, never getting over how absolutely fucking beautiful he was in the morning. He had that messy just-boned look, appropriate for what we did last night.

I pushed some of the blond back and he kissed my palm.

"I need to know everything," I pushed. "Everything that happened that night with Paige."

He had the answers, and he needed to give them to me, my right. That was my sister, and he knew more than he was allowing me to. So much was going on here, but I was here now, here to listen.

He played with my hair as well, each touch to dark tendrils shooting electrodes directly into my scalp. I eased into him for his smell and heat, unable to get enough.

"You don't know what you're asking," he stated, eventually cupping my cheek. "You just have no fucking idea."

Which was why I needed him to tell me. I took his hand, waiting.

He touched his brow to mine. "I don't want you to get hurt. What happened with Paige just starts with that night. It's deep, and even I don't have all the answers. I'm trying to figure it out, and it's getting darker and darker the deeper I go in."

I pushed arms around his waist, and he hugged me close.

He breathed into my hair. "I can't have you getting hurt."

"Can you?" I asked. "Is it possible... whatever this is, you might get hurt?"

He pulled away, pushing my hair back with a nod.

I wet my lips. "Then I'm all in. I need to know the truth, everything, and if something might happen to you too because of all this, I definitely need to know. What's going on?"

He embraced me with his long arms, muscled body and hard biceps wrapped around me. "I don't deserve you. And you didn't deserve this. You or Paige."

I swallowed, closing my eyes.

"This is going to get fucking deep, Em," he said. "It's gonna get worse, and that's not just a speculation. That's a promise. What the guys and I have unleashed is hell. We're at fucking Dante's gates, and who knows how worse that fire's going to get as we go deeper. It's bad. It's fucking sick."

I choked down a swallow again, and though I was scared

also, terrified of the unknown and what he could possibly be talking about, I'd stay brave. If he was going to go through the gates of hell, I would too. I'd do it for my sister.

I'd do it for him too.

His hand came down my neck, smoothing before resting between my breasts. He held a firm hand there, my heart racing against him.

"Where's Mallick's token?" he asked, returning his hand to my neck. "The necklace he gave you?"

I'd lied so well, hadn't I? A part of my own darkness. I took his hand. "All of that is over now. It was never real."

He put distance between us a little, looking at me and touching anywhere he could find skin. He couldn't seem to stop, doing that all night. "What do you mean?"

I chewed my lip. "Ramses speculated what was going on with you, the guys, and Paige at Route 80 before Christmas. That's how I found out. After, we had a plan for him to get into Court so we could figure out the truth and expose what happened to Paige. The relationship between us was a lie for that. Never real."

It was never... this, his hands on me, the feel of us together. It was so much more real than that and anything I'd ever felt with anyone else. This guy's touch brought me to life, and his darkness I found myself wanting to do anything but leave from. I wanted to balance him, put it out. He was a good person. He just needed that balance, and I fully believed that.

Fingers came up to my lips, his thumb parting them. "You're not his? Never was?"

"No..." I sighed, closing my eyes as he kissed me again. He sucked me into his heat, his body so close to mine. Eventually, I felt his hand go between us and to his own neck.

He unclasped it, removing a silver chain he wore. He had it on last night, and when he raised his hand between us, he slipped off his king ring.

He slid it on that chain, the chrome sinking right to the center with its weight. He looked at me after, lifting the chain and motioning toward my neck.

I moved my hair.

He put the chain around me, the metal warm on my skin.

"This doesn't mean you belong to me," he said, clasping the necklace before bringing the ring forward. He lifted the ring. "It means you're a part of me, a part of all this. I don't own you because you can't be owned."

Understanding, I closed my eyes, kissing him again. He pushed his weight on me, and I opened my legs for him. I didn't own him either.

We were a part of whatever we were about to embark on together.

CHAPTER
TWENTY-SEVEN

December

Arriving at school was different that day. Everything was different. Royal and I were somewhere else now, and since we'd arrived to that place, we weren't going back. Wherever we were headed, we were doing so together, unable to be parted. Not this time.

He kept his arm around me the whole journey to school, only leaving in the moments we stopped at my house so I could change and check in with my dad. Dad had actually been pretty lax about the whole, "not coming home" thing like he had before and didn't even question where I'd been. So much had changed, and I recalled Ramses' voice in my head.

"Maybe he does care… You never know until you let him."

This might have been him extending the olive branch, new levels to so many of my relationships lately. Thoughts traveled to Ramses and how I'd left things with him. He obviously suggested I'd go see Royal last night, but I hadn't told him I would. He clearly had some feelings for me, and though I didn't want to rub things in his face, I couldn't put distance between Royal and me. We showed up to school together, his arm still around me. In the busy halls, people definitely stared at us, but I didn't care. Like stated, we were in a different place now, and everything else didn't seem to matter. We managed to avoid confrontations with friends and everyone else on the way in, getting to his locker unscathed. There'd be time for those talks eventually, those moments later.

Dropping his arm from my shoulders, he grabbed my hips, pressing me against his locker. He didn't look at anything else but my mouth before kissing me right there in the traffic-filled hall, a kiss that literally made me forget everything else. After it was over, he kept his hands on my hips, pressing his forehead against mine.

"I can't tell you everything," he said. "Everything about Paige? It's something I have to... well, I have to show you."

I had no idea what this meant but decided to trust him, gripping his uniform's lapels. "Okay."

I said okay because *that's* where we were now. There were no more lies, only trust, and he tipped my chin, kissing me again.

He pulled back, his thumb brushing my skin. "We'll go after school since it's Friday, make a road trip of it. You'll know everything by the end. Everything I know. I promise."

The certainty of that scared me just as much as anything else, knowing not just the truth but whatever further darkness he felt was behind it. My sister dying had already been tragic the way I'd believed...

But for there to be more?

All of this may gut me in the end. I might not be strong enough, and as if knowing that, Royal pulled me away from the lockers. He brought an arm around me, kissing my hair, and I knew whatever this was, he'd stand by me. He'd get me through it, and he had me as well. I'd be there for him too.

"Hey, guys."

Royal touched our heads together briefly before lifting and finding Jax. He stood there, in his uniform as we were. He had his hands in his pockets, and the judgment I thought might be there at seeing Royal and me together was absent. Maybe he knew Royal and I ultimately coming together would happen. Maybe Royal had even told him while he'd been waiting for me to get ready when we stopped at my house that morning. I didn't know what Jax knew, but for whatever reason, him seeing Royal and me together didn't visibly bother him like I thought it might.

Royal left his arm around my neck, keeping me close. He might have said something, but Jax leaned in first.

Jax frowned. "The guys told me to get you—"

"Attention, student body of Windsor Preparatory Academy," came over the speaker, a female voice. I recognized the voice as Principal Hastings's secretary, Mrs. Norris. "We're having an assembly before first hour classes today. Please report to the central gymnasium immediately."

Everyone in the hallway immediately started to move that way, but Jax held us back.

"What's going on?" Royal asked, and when Jax looked at me, Royal held a hand up. "She's fine. Tell us both."

Nodding, Jax pushed hands in his pockets. "There's whispers surrounding the assembly. People are saying it's Mira."

Royal's eyebrows narrowed. "What is?"

"The assembly. Folks are saying *she's* the reason for it." He looked around before facing us. "They're saying she committed suicide."

Thank you so much for checking out COURT KEPT (Court High 3)! You can get the final book in the Court High saga, WE THE PRETTY STARS, on Amazon.

Did you know there's a website dedicated to all things Court High? There is and it features exclusive content you can't get anywhere else! The website exclusives include playlists, graphics, character bios/photos, and so much more!

Want access to the website? Simply subscribe to my newsletter! There, you'll get new release news from me and a link to the newsletter exclusive Court High website. What are you waiting for? Get access today! =^)

Website access: https://bit.ly/3v7nTu5

Made in the USA
Coppell, TX
11 March 2023